**What review**

MW01610216

### The Corrigan Women –

*In its rich and sometimes violent emotional texture, The Corrigan Women belongs in a class with such works as Alistair MacLeod's Lost Salt Gift of Blood.*

– New Maritimes

*If Dohaney never writes another novel, she can rest assured that her first has been worthwhile ... a convincing account of life in any Newfoundland cove.*

– Globe and Mail

*Dohaney's unfailing ear for dialogue and use of dark humour create characters almost too vibrant to be contained by the page.*

– Quill & Quire

### The Flannigans

*M.T. Dohaney's awareness of Newfoundland speech and her understanding of life in a deeply Catholic, pre-Confederation outport are used to good effect in this story of the swift and terrible disintegration of the Flannigan family.*

– Bernice Morgan

*Dohaney draws the characters and their emotions so finely that generations who weren't alive to witness (or are too young to remember) this turning point in our history can begin to imagine the intensity of that time.*

– Downhome

*For all that has been said and written, no one has ever come close to capturing the emotions of Confederation quite like M.T. (Jean) Dohaney has.*

– The Aurora

## Books by M.T. Dohaney

*The Corrigan Women* (a novel). Charlottetown, Prince Edward Island: Ragweed Press, 1988.

*To Scatter Stones.* Fredericton, New Brunswick: Goose Lane Editions, 1992.

*A Marriage of Masks.* Charlottetown, Prince Edward Island: Ragweed Press, 1995. (Winner of the Thomas Head Raddall Atlantic Fiction Prize, 1996.)

*When Things Get Back to Normal* (a memoir). Fredericton, New Brunswick: Goose Lane Editions, 2000.

*A Fit Month For Dying.* Fredericton, New Brunswick: Goose Lane Editions, 2000.

*The Flannigans: A Novel.* St. John's, Newfoundland and Labrador: Pennywell Press, 2007.

# Caplin Scull

**Chronicles from a
Newfoundland Outport
on the Eve of Confederation**

# M.T. Dohaney

Pottersfield Press, Lawrencetown Beach, Nova Scotia, Canada

Library and Archives Canada Cataloguing in Publication
Dohaney, M. T., 1930-
[Short stories. Selections]
Caplin Scull : chronicles from a Newfoundland outport
on the eve of confederation / by M.T. Dohaney.
Short stories.
ISBN 978-1-988286-09-9 (softcover)
I. Title.
PS8557.O257A6 2017   C813'.54           C2017-902854-5

Cover design: Gail LeBlanc

Pottersfield Press gratefully acknowledges the financial support of the Government of Canada through the Canada Book Fund for our publishing activities. We also acknowledge the support of the Canada Council for the Arts and the Province of Nova Scotia which has assisted us to develop and promote our creative industries for the benefit of all Nova Scotians.

Pottersfield Press
83 Leslie Road
East Lawrencetown, Nova Scotia, Canada, B2Z 1P8
Website: www.PottersfieldPress.com
To order, phone 1-800-NIMBUS9 (1-800-646-2879) www.nimbus.ns.ca

Printed in Canada
Pottersfield Press is committed to preserving the environment and the appropriate harvesting of trees and has printed this book on Forest Stewardship Council® certified paper.

RECYCLED
Paper made from
recycled material
FSC
www.fsc.org    FSC® C103567

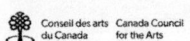
Conseil des arts   Canada Council
du Canada          for the Arts

Funded by the
Government
of Canada

Financé par le
gouvernement
du Canada

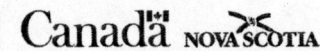
Canada   NOVA SCOTIA

*In Memory of my Father*

# Contents

# *Introduction*

Caplin Scull is not a true name, but it is a fitting one for the sea-lashed village on Newfoundland's east coast. The caplin scull is a yearly occurrence that takes place during the last two weeks in June and the first week in July. The caplin – small, silver, smelt-like fish – migrate from the deep sea and come to spawn on the beaches that surround the villages. Although they can come at any time of the day, the most common time is in the early morning hours. Whether the tiny fish intend to throw themselves in a hari-kari fashion upon the wind-thrashed shore is not fully understood. The most commonly accepted theory is that they are brought to shore by the ir-resistible tidal force of life: to spawn and die on the beaches and in so doing provide food for other fish – cod, herring, whales – and for humans as well. The males fertilize the spawn and then they, too, die, one

generation giving life to the next. It is an amazing example of the purpose-driven life.

As the caplin heave ashore, the fog thickens and
the foghorn blares almost non-stop. Why the heaving
ashore of caplin is always accompanied by heavy
fog, I do not know. I only know that in childhood,
the sound of the horses pulling the box carts loaded
with caplin in the fog-filled dawn was always an
assuring sign that we had survived the winter and
the life-sustaining summer was upon us: "God's in His
heaven; all's right with the world."

Most of the houses in Caplin Scull cling to the
cliffs that surround it. They look tired and woebe-
gone, as if they have had enough of eyeballing the
rough Atlantic Ocean, enough of having their clapboards gnawed clean of paint by the salty whitecaps
that blow over the beach, enough of the mournful
sound of the foghorn, enough of the battering wind
that seldom takes a break. Some of the houses that
do not cling to a cliff are scattered in meadows at
the base of it as if someone had flung a handful of
house seed to the wind and the houses had sprung
up willy-nilly.

My father taught me to love a good story. On
stormy days, when it wasn't fit for man nor beast to
go outside, he would sit on our kitchen floor beside
the stove and tell us children stories. While I loved
all of the stories – about lumber woods ghosts, train
wrecks, chimney fires that had been set by "the mischievous little people" – I particularly loved stories
about shipwrecks, and the comeuppance of those who
had deliberately lured vessels upon the rocks so they
could plunder and pillage them. What I most loved to

hear about were those saucy boats with more than a hint of liquor on their breath who were always able to outrun the U.S. Coast Guard. It is to him I dedicate this book of stories, each of which contains a kernel of truth, some more than a kernel.

## *The Summer of Lannie Ramunski*

In the soft moments of my life I can still hear her voice. It is husky. A smoker's voice, although at the time I met her she had only been smoking for a couple of months, and even then only on the sly, out of sight of her grandmother. Mrs. Furlong had no idea that her summer visitor never left her bedroom without her pack of Lucky's hidden in the waistband of her underwear.

Lannie had a quick, easy smile. It would light up her eyes, reminding me of the forget-me-nots that grew in our backyard. She wore her long blonde hair draped over one eye, á la Veronica Lake. Her mother, whose salad days had been spent in the '40s, and who knew everything there was to know about the movie stars of that time, had told her that there was even a song about Veronica Lake's hairdo. Sometimes Lannie would sing a few bars of "A Sweater, a Sarong, and a Peekaboo Bang" just to demonstrate that the information she was parcelling out was correct. At fifteen, I was certain that had I been given a hand in fashioning myself, and I would have gladly become a clone of Lannie Ramunski.

But I have other memories of Lannie as well. Sad memories. I was with her on the day she learned her mother had died on the operating table while undergoing an operation for cancer. Her anguished cry when she read the telegram her father had sent her from Boston is still as fresh in my memory as if no years have intervened. It is a piercing shrill sound that rises and falls like the screech of a seagull. And I can still see her crumpled form as she lay huddled at the foot of her bed, a broken creature, her hand clutching the telegram. I hadn't read the telegram and I wondered how her father had worded his condolences since he had abandoned both wife and daughter many years earlier.

From the instant my school mates and I learned Lannie Ramunski was going to be spending the summer in our village – a small, isolated, sea-battered clutch of houses backed up against a barren cliff – we were filled with titillating intrigue and exquisite anticipation. Just her name alone resonated with a ring of outlandishness. For some of us it even teetered on the brink of damnation.

Sister Ignatius, our tenth-grade teacher, confirmed that her research showed there never had been a Saint Lannie. A shocking revelation for us to be sure! Without a heavenly benefactor to intercede for her, who could she call upon to coax and wheedle favours from God on her behalf? Who, indeed!

Sr. Ignatius said that Lannie was more likely a trumped-up Hollywood name, and her lip curled when she said the word Hollywood. She dispensed this information as she flicked her waist-length black serge veil over her shoulder with one hand, while with the other she held a book of saints and martyrs splayed open on her desk. She ran her index finger down the list of names to see if she could find one from which "Lannie" could be derived, no matter how remote the connection. But there was neither saint nor martyr whose name came even close.

She then slammed the book shut and rapped her knuckles on its cover to signal her search was now completed.

"Like a favourite aunt," she explained, as if we needed an explanation as to the significance of having a saintly namesake. "The saints reside at God's right hand." As she said this, she indicated with her own pale right hand the proximity of God to the saints. She pointed from one side of her desk to the other, measuring the distance. "From their lips to. His ear is only a whisper away." At this point her voice would drop so low we could barely make out her words.

"How wonderful it must be to be so close to the Lord." There was such reverence in her voice that her lower lip trembled, and at that moment every girl in the classroom would have gladly given her life then and there for a chance at beatification and our pity for Lannie Ramunski was boundless. "The poor soul," we thought. "No one to intercede for her."

Other than Lannie, our soon-to-be visitor, we knew of no one who was in such a precarious situation. Certainly, no one in our village was without a saint's name. Every morning when Sr. Ignatius called roll, it sounded as if she were reading straight from the Litany of the Saints and they were all Irish at that.

There was Mary, Agnes, and Mary Agnes. There was Lucy, Cecilia, Ann, Elizabeth, Sarah, Rose, Catherine, Paul, James, Ambrose, Steven, Patrick, John. In case of duplication, other distinctions had to be made. Elizabeth from the Gulch. Elizabeth from the Harbour. Patrick from Up Along. Patrick from the Cove. And of course, there were diminutives: Betsy, Betty, and Liz; Paddy, Pad, and Pat.

Our saints' namesakes had been given to us at our baptism. Some parents – the more fervent ones – had given their children two saints' names. I had been given three. However, to take credit for three – Mary Magdalene Theresa – I had to separate Mary from Magdalene and accept that Magdalene, being that she was only listed as a Holy Woman, had never been elevated to sainthood. And I had to discount the fact that I was called Theresa, not to honour the saint who dropped flowers from heaven, but to honour my grandmother – a crusty old woman who was still in this world and definitely no candidate for sainthood.

With our particular bent of mind, however, it is therefore understandable why it was appalling to us to learn that our upcoming summer visitor lacked a heavenly benefactor. And the foreign sounding nature of her surname – Ramunski – only compounded our distress. Ramunski had a definite heathen ring to it. Our surnames could be traced back to generations of ancestors who had come to Newfoundland directly from Ireland – St. Patrick's Ireland: O'Rourke, O'Brien, O'Sullivan, O'Reilly, Clancy, Cleary, Callaghan, Conway, Kelly, Dunphy, Daugherty, Foley, Finnigan, and Furlong. There wasn't a Smith or a Jones in the group, much less a name as outlandish as Ramunski.

I was one of the first to learn about Lannie's upcoming visit and I lost no time in spreading this news about. The information had come to me via eavesdropping on a conversation between my mother and Mrs. Furlong, Lannie's grandmother. Mrs. Furlong was our neighbour and one Saturday morning when she and my mother were sitting in the kitchen having a cup of tea, I came downstairs from my bedroom to retrieve a sweater I had left hanging over a chair beside the table. Just before I entered the kitchen, I overheard a snippet of their conversation which piqued my interest so much that I did not immediately make my presence known. Instead, I hovered outside the door, out of sight, but near enough to hear Mrs. Furlong relate news about her daughter who was living in Boston and her granddaughter, Lannie, who was living with her.

"She's having a heavy operation, girl," she said, referring to her daughter, revealing the contents of a letter her daughter had written to her and which she had picked up at the post office on Friday afternoon. "On her womanly parts. She already had some work done last year. Remember? I told you about it back then. They took out the part where the cancer had set in. Now 'tis back agin. In another place of course."

"The poor soul," my mother responded, dropping her voice in the way she always did whenever she talked about bad news having befallen someone. "And was that what her letter was all about?"

"Yes, partly. And she wants to know if I'm up to having her girl come live with me for the summer."

"Oh my, Mrs.," Mother prophesied dourly. "A lot of responsibility, m'am. And you not well yerself."

"Yer right in that regard, girl. Of course, I'm not up to it. Me heart hardly got enough push in it to hold me upright these days. But what can I do? Can't leave the girl alone. She's only fifteen. Same age as your Theresa. And a father not worth a pinch of hen shit. As you knows very well, Fred Ramunski slipped the traces a couple of years ago and traipsed off with another woman, leaving Gloria and Lannie to fend for themselves."

She shrugged indifferently. "I think it was with a woman who worked in the funeral parlour business with him. But what does it matter who it was. Gloria called her the Undertaker Hag. She said Fred and this hag used to get soused together on embalming fluid. But she may have made that up. Gloria was always inclined to stretch things."

"Oh, I remember when he jumped the fence," my mother confirmed. "Or at least when he got caught jumping the fence. Can't say I was surprised. Right from the first I had him pegged as a gallivant. But Gloria couldn't see beyond the uniform. She was determined to get herself an American serviceman so she could go live in the States."

"Fer sure. Yer right on that, too, girl. I felt the same way as you did about him. Blood of a bitch, that's what he is. If I could get me hands on him, I'd rip out his privates so he'd have no reason to gallivant. No reason to jump the fences."

They both laughed at her bawdiness and then moved on with their conversation about the granddaughter's visit.

As soon as Mrs. Furlong left our house that morning I asked my mother for more details on Lannie Ramunski. Just her name alone had already captured my imagination. And because we would be neighbours I was certain she would be my special friend. I was sure I would be the envy of the other girls in my class who often cliqued together and snubbed me because their houses were situated farther up the road. They were lined up cheek to jowl, allowing them to frequently visit each other.

But there was also the excitement of spending a summer with someone who was from that magical place called Boston. I had aunts and uncles who were living there and although I had never met any of them, their Christmas and Easter and birthday cards were always so filled with enchantment that I would stare at them for hours. I saved each one. These cards decorated our Christmas tree year after year. They had tinsel and ribbon and embossed printing and glitter that came off on your fingers and sparkled like fairy dust.

Our own cards were church bought and they were unadorned and with a predictable religious theme. At Christmas there was the Manger scene. At Easter there was The Last Supper. And on St. Patrick's Day there was St. Patrick himself in his green bishop's robes with a few slain snakes lying prone at his feet. But there was never any glitter. Nor tinsel. Nor embossing. Nor ribbons. And certainly no extravagantly brilliant colours.

"How many times do I have to tell you to stop snooping in on other people's conversation?" Mother asked, sidestepping my urgent need for details about Lannie. "I keep telling you that people who eavesdrop never hear anything good about themselves."

"I didn't hear anything bad about myself," I peevishly countered, knowing she was embarrassed because I had overheard her laughing at Mrs. Furlong's bawdy talk. "You were talking about this Lannie person. And about her mother. And about her father. Nothing about me. So I heard nothing bad about myself."

"Well, one of these days, my lady," she predicted with a turndown of her lips and immediately began a tirade on what was really on her mind.

"I'm telling you now," she said, wagging her finger in the direction of Betsy Furlong's house, "I've got enough to do this summer with your father only able to get home on weekends without having to take on the worry of you. So I don't want you hanging around with this girl this summer if she turns out to be a wild one. I don't care even if it puts Betsy's nose out of shape. Those girls from Boston can be as hard as nails. And this one never had a father to guide her."

She continued on in this vein, ending with her strongest suit as to why I should not take up with Mrs. Furlong's American granddaughter. "And as far

as I can tell she's not even Christian, much less Catholic because that husband of hers forbid her to have
the child baptized. Betsy once told me that she wanted Gloria to sneak the child into a church to get her
baptized or even dunk her in the kitchen sink herself
because that's acceptable in extreme cases. But Gloria did nothing except lament in her letters. She was
afraid of that husband, I suppose. He said the bap-
tizing stuff was all nonsense and he didn't want any
part of it. Myself, I would have cheeked right up to
him and said, 'If 'tis all nonsense like you think 'tis,
why not let me get her baptized, just to humour me?
If it's just foolishness, what's the harm?'"

Mother gave a defiant toss of her head, leaving no doubt that Gloria's husband would not easily
get around her had she been the one married to him.
And there would be no furtive dunking in the kitchen
sink either.

"At least that makes sense to me," she continued. "I say why should he fear something that he believes is just a bunch of nonsense? Poor old Selena
Cleary believed that stepping on a crack would break
her mother's back, so she spent a lifetime dodging
potholes and frost heaves. But what harm if that's
what she believed. Didn't hurt us any to see her
jumping about like a grasshopper. And it helped *her*.
Much the same with having this child baptized. If he
believed it was all nonsense, it couldn't have done
any damage just to have a drop of water sprinkled on
her head. And it would have meant so much to her
grandmother."

All of Mother's chatter only served to make me
more inquisitive about Lannie, but none of it pre-

pared me for that first breathtaking sight of her. Nor did it protect me from becoming completely enthralled with her.

She was tall, but not gangly tall. She had shoulder-length yellow hair. I was to learn that her hair colour had been helped along by a bottle of peroxide. She told me this unabashedly as if bleaching one's hair wasn't the stuff of a Jezebel. Her skin was cream-coloured, and in comparison, our ruddy, sea-cured cheeks seemed common and vulgar.

And the clothes she wore were all gaily coloured – saucy clothes, Mother said – but they made our paltry wardrobes, especially our black school uniforms, seem so dull and dowdy, so work-a-day. She wore her cardigan-style sweaters with the sleeves pushed up to the elbows and always with the buttons in the back, unashamedly displaying her breasts that were just in a state of becoming.

Her full, waltz-length cotton skirts were the height of fashion – a fashion we had only been privy to in an Eaton's catalogue. The skirts billowed out with the help of several underslips of fine, white netting, which she called crinolines. I never tired of seeing the swish of skirt and netting as she picked her way over rocky beaches and narrow paths that were littered with sheep dung. She wore lipstick – pale pink lipstick – and nail polish to match. Compared to my unvarnished flesh, this was pure Mary Magdalene before her redemption.

I fell instantly in love with Lannie and my mother's severe warning to keep my distance fell on deaf ears. My powerful crush on Anthony Callaghan vanished like the fog before a gale-force wind. My future plans to be a nurse waned, and no longer did I feel the need to be in the good graces of the girls in my class. I wanted only to be metamorphosed into a dizzyingly delightful Lannie Ramunski. I wanted all of her qualities to be my qualities and if this was beyond being attainable, I was willing to settle for being caught forever in the orbit of her sweep.

I mimicked Lannie's accent until my mouth got stiff from the effort. *We pawked the caw in the pawking lot.* I also practised her walk and the way she tossed her head, her hair swinging sultrily with each toss from her left shoulder to right. But all of my mimicking was of no avail. Sensual and sexy continued to elude me. Uniforms made of black serge worn two inches below the knee, accompanied by round-toed, flat-heeled black shoes and hair chopped close to the ear line were never meant to lend themselves to a provocative image.

Anthony Callaghan didn't pine very long over my withdrawn affections. He also fell head over heels in love with Lannie. From the moment he set eyes upon her, all romantic thoughts of me seemed to have vaporized. He no longer wanted to sit beside me whenever we huddled in groups on the bank of the brook that ran through our village. And if it got chilly, it was Lannie to whom he offered his sweater.

I blamed only Anthony for this humiliating betrayal. How could I blame Lannie if Anthony had honed in on her? Can you blame the wild rose for attracting a bee, or the light bulb for enticing the moth? Besides, Lannie had told me that she had a real boyfriend back home and Anthony was only a summer fling and I could have him back as soon as she left for Boston. She showed me a photograph of this Boston boyfriend to reassure me that this was so, and I could see at a glance that Anthony was no match for the Jimmy Dean look-alike who stared sulkily into the camera.

Lannie not only sensed my need to be refashioned into her image, but she was willing to help bring this about. She would always offer to loan me her lipsticks that she had lined up on Mrs. Furlong's bureau, like sentries at a castle.

"Try this one," she would say, pushing a lipstick up out of its shiny gold case, a tower of exquisite and tantalizing rose pink. I could almost taste the glycerine sliding over my lips, and I could imagine pressing my lips together, the way Lannie did, to spread the colour evenly. But I always refused. I could not take the chance of having my mother find out what I had done, thereby giving her cause to forbid me to hang around with Lannie. To insure my continued association with her, I knew I had to be a paragon of virtue, a model of decorum. Mother did not give second chances.

One evening, however, when Mother and Mrs. Furlong had gone to a church card party, Lannie snatched the opportunity to set loose the siren that cowered inside me, hungering for escape. She announced she was going to make me glamorous.

She had seen my wardrobe and knew that nothing in it would be of any help. School uniforms and wool sweaters made from black homespun yarn do not a temptress make even in the hands of an expert like Lannie. She offered up her own clothes.

She pulled a white cardigan from its hanger

and began buttoning it up on me – buttons in back, of course – commenting as she worked that she had tons of sweaters because before her mother had gotten sick, she had worked in the basement of Filene's Department Store and was permitted a ten percent store discount. As well, she had always bought clothes for the two of them from the marked-down rack, which by the third markdown cost little or nothing. To complement the sweater, she added a cotton skirt with two crinolines and then styled my hair so one side fell over my eye. The glistening pink lipstick was the final touch.

I surveyed my startling new image in the mirror. Because I had no breasts to speak of – Anthony once quipped that I was a carpenter's dream, a flat board – the back-to-front sweater made me look as if my head was on backwards. But despite this body flaw, my first look at my renovated self almost took my breath away. When I pushed up the sweater sleeves and pirouetted on my round-toed black brogues, I was staggered by the change. No caterpillar had ever surveyed her butterfly transformation with more astonishment, with more delight. Vanity aside, I knew I outshone all other girls in the village – all except Lannie.

From then on, my days were filled with exhilarating intrigue and heart-stopping scheming. The night hours were of no account because they were hours without Lannie, and like Lady Macbeth, sleep was simply a means of knitting up the ravelled sleeve of care, which took the form of wardrobe changes. The skirts, the crinolines, the lipstick, the back-to-front sweaters, and eventually even the nail polish were now an everyday event and all of this had to be done surreptitiously at Mrs. Furlong's house.

Because her health was deteriorating, Mrs. Furlong spent most of her days lying on the couch in her kitchen listening to the soap serials on the radio and taking little interest in our comings and goings. Each time we dodged her inspection, we felt giddy with relief as if we had just made our escape from Alcatraz. When we would get outdoors and the real and present danger was safely thwarted, we would break into gales of muffled laughter.

But not all of our moments together were so high-spirited. Sometimes when we were alone our conversations would take a more reflective and wistful direction. One day, as we were sitting on the bank beside the brook and letting our bare feet dangle in the water, Lannie said, apropos nothing that had to do with our conversation at hand, that I was lucky because my father loved me. It seemed to me to be such a senseless remark because speculating on whether or not my parents loved me was a thought so foreign, so alien to my world that I had never even entertained it. Weren't parents supposed to love you? That was their God-given duty. It was not a thought that I had ever had need to ponder.

However, because she, herself, had tabled the discussion on parents, I felt free to ask the question that I had not dared bring up earlier.

"Why do you always call your father Undertaker Fred? Why not Dad or Father?"

Her answer was clear and simple and, to her, obvious.

"Because he owns a funeral parlour."

It was not so obvious to me. "My father is a

fisherman, but he's still my father. I wouldn't think of calling him Fisherman Jim."

"Your father didn't leave your mother and you for a 'Bit of Stuff.'" She said this in a tone that conveyed to me that I should have known that her father's leaving her for a Bit of Stuff had cancelled their relationship.

"*Bit of Stuff?* You mean a girlfriend?"

"Yeah, that's what Mother calls her. Or Fred's Folly. Behind her back, of course. But not behind Undertaker Fred's back. It really galls him when she calls the Bit of Stuff names. I always call her Mag the Hag. Her first name is Maggie. That makes Undertaker Fred furious."

"Is she nice?"

"Do nice women break up families?"

I shrugged. I hadn't ever known such a woman. Or even known of such a woman. She accepted the shrug and continued.

"I've never met her. And don't plan on meeting her either. And I hardly ever see him. If Grandmother hadn't taken me this summer, he would have been forced to take me. I told Mom I'd do away with myself first." She made a motion as if she were slitting her throat.

"Don't even joke about that!" I admonished, half in jealous anger that she could so easily leave me behind in death and half in morbid fear that she would go to hell and I would never be reunited with her. "Don't you know that it's a mortal sin to take your own life?"

"A mortal sin? Never heard of such a thing! I always thought a sin was a sin."

I proceeded to educate her. "No. There's venial sins and mortal sins."

She flashed a mischievous grin. "You mean they grade sins. Like eggs. Grade A. Grade B."

She then swished her hair over her shoulder, and made a terrifying pronouncement. "If I'd rather be dead than live with Mag the Hag, that's my business. Not anyone else's. Not even God's."

I instantly went to great lengths to explain what I had been taught about suicide – that it is slapping God's gift of life in His face and because there is no chance of asking forgiveness, hell is a certainty.

"Get on!" she said, her eyes glinting mischievously. "You don't really believe that stuff, do you?"

The look on my face said I did and not wishing to explore the subject any further, she immediately switched the topic to one of Fred's undertaker jokes.

"What did one casket say to the other in the dead of night in the funeral parlour?"

"I've no idea," I said, short-toned, miffed at my profound conversation being dismissed so cavalierly.

She giggled and then supplied the answer. "Is that you coffin?"

When I knelt by the side of my bed that night, I released Mary Magdalene from her duty as my intercessor and turned her over to Lannie. I thought Magdalene would be better able to understand Lannie than would Theresa, my second intercessor. She would be less likely to be shocked by Lannie's irreverence. After all, she, herself, had had a sullied past and even had seven devils cast out of her. But despite her less than pure life, she had been present at the Crucifixion and at the Empty Tomb. I concluded from this that she must have been looked upon as a favourite and, therefore, she would be in a better position than others to save Lannie from the fires of hell. And in a roundabout way to save me from the intolerable pain of being separated from her forever.

\* \* \* \* \*

The telegram from her father arrived the day after her mother's operation had been scheduled. Her mother had died on the operating table. It was the last week in August. A Thursday. Mrs. Furlong's grandfather clock struck the hour as I passed through her kitchen on the way up to Lannie's room. Eleven mournful strikes.

"She's beside herself," Mrs. Furlong said when I walked into Lannie's room, stopping her own crying long enough to point to Lannie, who was crouched on the floor beside her open suitcase, the telegram in her hand wet from her tears.

"'Tis terrible, that's what 'tis," Mrs. Furlong lamented. "A sorrow too great to bear. And I'm not well enough to travel to the funeral, even if I had the money."

\* \* \* \* \*

Lannie left for Boston the following morning and my life instantly emptied. My days became hollow. The impending school year held no interest for me. Anthony tried to forge his way back into my affections, but I cast him away without a backward look, cast him out just as the devils had been cast out of Mary Magdalene. Over the summer my hair had grown to shoulder length and I had defied my mother by not having it cut. I now could swish it back and forth, chin lifted, head turned in haughty profile. Almost without my noticing, my breasts began showing signs that I wouldn't be a carpenter's dream forever. But all of this no longer brought me any joy.

\* \* \* \* \*

Quickly on the heels of Lannie's departure, more news arrived from Boston. It started with a whisper that went up and down the rows of desks in Sr. Ignatius' class. Sarah had gone to the convent to get coloured chalk for Sr. Ignatius. Mother Superior told her that a priest in Boston had called our parish priest with the news that Lannie Ramunski was dead and he was to inform Mrs. Furlong. As the story went, Lannie had a headache and she swallowed pain pills that she had brought from her mother's house when she went to live with her father. Unaware of their potency, she had accidentally taken too many.

I was stunned. So stunned that Sr. Ignatius had to tell me three times to get down on my knees to pray the De Profundis on behalf of Lannie's soul.

As I knelt on the hardwood floor and mumbled along with the others, *Out of the depths, I have cried to Thee, O Lord, Lord hear my voice,* I thought what a useless exercise this was. Lannie was beyond the reach of prayer.

I staggered to my feet and stumbled to the washroom. I sat on the toilet and beseeched every saint I could call to mind to intercede with God on

Lannie's behalf. In a special way I called upon Mary Magdalene. And then, because I had always been one to hedge my bets, I went directly to the Deity. "Please, God," I begged, "just this one time make an exception to Your suicide rule. You, alone, know how much she hated living with Undertaker Fred and Mag the Hag."

## A Meeting with the Devil

A February snowstorm in full rage – northeast wind, drifting snow, and temperatures low enough to freeze the marrow in one's bones – was well underway in every crevice and corner of Father O'Reilly's parish. With every gust of wind the rectory, where he was sleeping, see-sawed on its foundation. Its windows rattled in their puttied frames.

Father O'Reilly slept soundly in his feather bed, heaped up as it was with a mound of homemade quilts. At least he had been sleeping soundly until a minute or two earlier when he had been awakened by someone calling his name. The instant he heard it, he cocked his ear above the quilts and listened. He could hear no sound other than the wailing of the storm. He settled back down in bed, convinced it had been the wind that pulled him from his sleep. No one, he assured himself, would be out on such a night. He groped with his toes for the beach rock at the foot of his bed. It was still warm. That meant it couldn't be more than two o'clock.

"Fadder! Fadder 'Reilly!"

There it was again! He raised his head a few inches from the pillow and really concentrated on listening. He was an old man and he knew his mind sometimes played tricks on him.

"Fadder! Fadder 'Reilly!"

There was no mistaking it this time. Someone was calling his name! He hurriedly tossed the quilts off himself, got out of bed, and padded across the cold floor to the front-facing window that was always kept in working order for occasions such as this. He tried to peer out through one of the narrow panes of glass, but the heavy coating of frost made that impossible. He then put his shoulder to the window frame and pushed upward with all of his strength. The window edged up several inches. He shouted through this opening.

"Who's there?"

"'Tis me, Fadder. John Peter Foley from Barrachoix." The boy's voice, like Father O'Reilly's, was thick with the accent of forefathers who had come to Newfoundland from Ireland centuries earlier.

"It's who? Shout out – I can't hear ye!"

"John Peter Foley, Fadder. Robert's John's son."

"What's up, b'y? What's the trouble?"

"Me fadder. He seys he's dyin'."

Father O'Reilly breathed a sigh of relief. It was only Robert's John looking for attention again. "Ah sher, me son, there's nothing to get alarmed about. Yer father's been dyin' ever since I came to this parish and that's more than twenty year ago."

"I knows that, Fadder. But I thinks he means to go this time. He's been askin' for ye all evening."

"What does he say ails him now?"

"I don't know, Fadder. He went to bed around eight and said he was dyin' and kept askin' for ye. Said Old Nick would get his soul if you didn't hear his Confession."

Robert's John lived in Barrachoix, several miles beyond Placentia, even several miles beyond the village of Caplin Scull through which you had to pass en route to Barrachoix. The road to Barrachoix snaked around the shoreline of the Atlantic Ocean. It was narrow and potholed, making it treacherous for a horse, particularly on such a night. Father O'Reilly had made many false-alarm deathbed trips to Robert's John's house only to find out he was healthier than he was himself. And it was always on stormy nights such as this one.

"'Tis just a touch of flu he has, b'y," he assured John Peter. The words were sucked out of his mouth by the gale of wind almost before he had time to pronounce them. "Everyone's got it. I'll come out after early Mass in the morning."

But John Peter would not be put off. "Oh, but ye have to come right now, Fadder. I have the horse and sleigh so I can take ye and bring ye back. Fadder seys he really needs ye."

Father O'Reilly did not respond. He was thinking up more reasons why he was going to refuse to go with John Peter. He was old – too old for the job of serving the scattered parish of Placentia. But the bishop couldn't find anyone to replace him.

And as well as being old, he was very tired. He

had heard Confessions all evening. He had three Masses to say in the morning. Barrachoix was seven miles away and in the middle of nowhere. And besides all of those reasons, Robert's John had been saying for years that he was dying. Especially on stormy nights. It was at such times that he remembered the many fishing vessels he had lured upon the rocks with a false light. And it was then that he always wanted the priest. Father O'Reilly recalled that last month when he went out to see him after one of his urgent requests, Mrs. Cleary in Caplin Scull had died of a stroke while he was gone and she never got to receive the Last Rites.

"I won't go tonight, John Peter. But in the morning I will. I'll even cancel the early Mass." He paused, adding as an afterthought, "And take care, me son. 'Tis a lonely road. And some bad night out there."

\* \* \* \* \*

Father O'Reilly stayed by the window until the last sounds of the sleigh faded away. He then crawled back into his comfortable bed and searched with his feet for the warm beach rock that was wrapped in towels at the foot of his bed. But no matter how comfortable he got, he could not get back to sleep. Disturbing thoughts raced through his mind.

*What if Robert's John was really dying!*

He argued with himself. "*Sher I'm older than Robert's John. I expect he'll put me in the boneyard. Not the other way around.*"

*But what if he's really dying?*

He answered his own question. *"Nonsense, O'Reilly. He's always dying. And frightened to death to meet his Maker. And from what I've been hearing, with good reason."*

Frost rents cracked through the rectory like rifle shots. Father O'Reilly shivered. Even though the bed was weighted down with quilts and warm beach rocks and he was wearing his homespun underwear, he was still bone-chillingly cold.

"'Tis some wicked night," he thought, as a surge of wind once again rattled the windowpanes. Fast on the heels of this thought was another one. *"That's the real reason, isn't it? That's why you didn't go to Barrachoix. You think too much of your own comfort. You're not much of a priest, William Patrick O'Reilly, if you let your creature comforts get in the way of administering the Sacraments. Not much of a priest at all."*

He hurriedly threw back the quilts and jumped to his feet. He lit the kerosene lamp on his bedside table and then began to pull on his clothes. While still buttoning his flannel shirt, he picked up the lamp and made his way down the stairs and out through the cold corridor to the church to get a Consecrated Host from the tabernacle. As he rushed along the corridor, he noticed the frost on the nailheads that had popped through the boards.

"'Tis some night," he thought. "Some wicked night!"

On his way back from the church, he stopped by his tiny office just off the visitors' parlour to get his sick-call kit and then he proceeded to the back porch where he pulled on his overcoat and his double-knit mitts and fur cap with earflaps. Dressed for the weather, he made his way to the stable to harness the horse.

\* \* \* \* \*

The road to Barrachoix was little more than a trail that twisted and turned to avoid boulders and wind-stripped trees. Sometimes there was nothing in sight but the North Atlantic Ocean to his right and stretches of naked bog to his left. But by this time Father O'Reilly was not concerned with the road. He sat hunched on his sleigh trying to coax more speed from his horse that was almost as old and tired as he was.

Snowdrifts swirled around the sleigh and down the priest's neck and up his coat sleeves. His hands became so numb he could barely clutch the whip, which he used to urge the frightened animal to move faster through the snow.

The village of Barrachoix consisted of five houses hunched together at the edge of a cliff. As Father O'Reilly came close to Robert's John's house, he saw that there was lamplight coming from an upstairs window. Light from a lamp was also coming from the kitchen window. And from the parlour window. Through the frost-covered glass he could see shadows moving around inside.

"Thanks be to God, I came," he muttered to himself as he awkwardly lumbered out of the sleigh. "He must be in really bad shape or they wouldn't be up at this hour."

Without even taking the time to throw a blanket over the sweating horse, he rushed up the snow-clogged walk to the kitchen door. He entered without knocking, as was the custom of the area. John Peter was in the kitchen stoking up the wood stove.

"'Tis you, Fadder 'Reilly," John Peter gasped in surprise when he saw the priest standing in the centre of the kitchen, whiskers of frost clinging to his day-old beard. Then he lowered his voice almost to a whisper and said, "But yer too late! Me fadder is dead."

Father O'Reilly's knees buckled and he steadied himself by clutching the kitchen table. "When did he die?" he asked.

"Just this minute, Fadder. Just this blessed minute. We jest came down from his bedroom. Me mudder is in the parlour getting it ready for the wake."

"He was alive then when you got back?"

"He was, Fadder. If ye had come with me, he'd have been alive when ye got here."

Father O'Reilly rushed for the door leading to the upstairs. "I might still be in time," he said, more to console himself than to comfort John Peter.

\* \* \* \* \*

Robert's John lay in the bed, his eyes still open and staring into space. Father O'Reilly bent to administer the Last Rites.

"But he's dead, Fadder," John Peter, who had followed him up the stairs, protested. "What's the good of doing that when he's already dead?"

"You can never tell for sure, me son. Sometimes when they look dead, there's some life left."

But Father O'Reilly knew he was only trying to

convince himself. Robert's John was as dead as last
year's caplin that drove upon the beach in June. He
straightened up from bending over the body and said
wearily, "'Tis a pity I didn't come when ye called to
me, John Peter."

"'Tis indeed, Fadder. He kept asking for ye to
the bitter end. He kept saying he wanted to confess
his sins because he was going straight to hell if he
didn't."

"But I heard his confession last month when he
thought he was dying."

"Not the same, Fadder. Seems he had a sin he
held onto until the last minute. Least that's what he
said to Mudder. All the other times he banked on getting better and making do with a half-confession."

Father O'Reilly winced as John Peter related how
his father had begged for the Last Rites. He was well
aware it was his fault that Robert's John had died
without receiving them. And if he was in hell, then
he was the one who had helped put him there. It was
concern for his own comforts that had allowed him to
play directly into the Devil's hands. He could almost
hear Old Nick laughing at him. He tried to push such
thoughts away, but they wouldn't budge from his
mind.

"I'll be going now, John Peter," he said. "I have
Masses to say in a couple of hours. Tell yer poor
mother I was here. I'll be on hand for the funeral
Mass."

John Peter extended his hand. "Thanks fer
comin', Fadder. I'll get me coat and boots and go with
ye to help get the horse underway."

The horse was tethered to the gatepost. Its

body was still covered with sweat which in spots had turned to ice. Whenever the poor creature moved it did so stiffly.

"He's worn out, Fadder," John Peter said. "Why don't you unharness him and put him in the stable for a while? Come back in and wait until daylight."

Father O'Reilly was tempted to go back inside, but he knew he had already neglected his duty by not getting on that sleigh with John Peter.

"There's no time, me son," he said. "Mass is at seven. I've got to get going."

He threw himself up on the sleigh and urged the horse out of the village.

The snowstorm had eased up, but the wind was still high and it was still bitterly cold. As he drove along, he fantasized having left the rectory the moment John Peter called, that he had been at Robert's John's side before he died, that Robert's John had been very happy to have the Last Rites. He even imagined giving him assurance that the devil wouldn't get him.

"Are ye sure, Fadder?" Robert's John had whispered near the end. "Are ye really sure the old Divil won't get me? I've done some things that would please *Himself* but not God."

"He's a forgiving God," he had assured him, "and now that you've made your peace with Him, Satan won't ..."

At that instant the horse stopped so suddenly Father O'Reilly lurched forward in the sleigh. He straightened up and looked around him. He was passing through a little cove where at one time the devil was supposed to have appeared to a priest and it was said that at that time Old Nick had left his footprint on a rock and that a well had sprung up beside the rock and it never went dry no matter how scarce the rainfall. Father O'Reilly himself had seen what appeared to be a hoof mark in the rock, but whether the Devil had made it or not he couldn't say. He rattled the reins to get the horse moving, but the animal paid no attention.

He shook the reins again, this time with more force, and the horse struggled forward a few paces and drew up sharply, its head turned sideways as if someone was holding it by its bridle.

"God Almighty!" Father O'Reilly gasped and cracked the whip hard. Fear crawled along his spine. He rapidly made the sign of the cross over himself several times.

"Let go!" he shouted. "Let go in God's name!" He jerked the reins. "Let go in God's name!"

The horse still did not move. He repeated the order once more, but the animal stayed rooted to the spot, its head remaining sideways.

"Let go in the Devil's name," he finally said. The horse's head instantly straightened as if the hold on it had been released. It lurched forward and kept going.

\* \* \* \* \*

Later that morning, Father O'Reilly appeared white and shaken on the altar in his parish church. When the Mass ended he turned to his parishioners, including my grandmother who related this story to me. He said, "Brethren, as I'm sure ye noticed I had no sermon today. But there is something I need to tell you."

Then he folded his hands beneath his vestments and told the story of the night's happenings.

"Three times," he said, holding up his fingers up for the count. "Three times I shouted, 'Let go in God's name!' But nothing happened. Then I said – and God forgive me for saying it – 'Let go in the Devil's name.'"

He shivered visibly. "I can still hear the screaming in my ears as my horse picked up his pace."

He then placed his hands over his ears as if he still could hear the awful sound. As he did so, he fell in a heap to the floor. An altar boy rushed over to the priest's side.

"Are ye all right, Fadder? Speak up, Fadder."

There was no response. Father O'Reilly was dead.

Father O'Reilly is buried in Mount Carmel cemetery, familiarly known as Dickson's Hill. This cemetery, which overlooks the town of Placentia on the east coast of Newfoundland, also serves the needs of several small communities in the area, Caplin Scull being one of them. Father O'Reilly's grave marker still stands today, and although the inscription has been worn away by the winds of many years, the words *Rest in Peace* are still clearly visible.

## *Fairy Lantern*

In the summer of the year I turned seven, a light appeared in our back pasture. I could see this light from my bedroom window. Father said it was a fairy lantern the little people used so they could prepare their supper after dark.

From that moment onward, my days and my nights were filled with enchantment. I would hurriedly eat my supper so I could sit by my bedroom window and watch for this light to appear. My every thought became focused on the leprechauns whom I imagined were stepping sprightly in the area of the light as they went about preparing their supper. If I held my breath so that all sound was stilled, I could almost hear them singing their fairy songs as they held hands and danced around the light. If I pressed my face so close to the window that my nose was flattened, I could almost see what they were eating. My culinary imagination didn't wander far from my own supper staples – baked beans, potato hash, or salt beef and cabbage. Or herring and boiled potatoes. Sometimes codfish and brewis, this latter a mixture of sea biscuit which had been softened in water and fried in fat that had been rendered out from salt pork.

Eventually, I became so overly stimulated by this routine that I was nearing a point of exhaustion and my father had to take me out into the back pasture after dark and show me that the fairy lantern was nothing more than the moonlight shining on a rotting stump.

The magic instantly evaporated. I was sad, but I was also glad. My obsession, as heady as it had been, had become a burden.

I now liken being newly in love to a fairy lantern. It is a compelling, tantalizing light in a distant meadow. It cannot, however, withstand an up-close or constant inspection without losing its allure. This, unfortunately, is as it must be. Ordinary mortals cannot withstand sustained enchantment.

They can, however, withstand the memory of those moments. Years and years later a certain sound, a certain breeze, a certain smell on a certain moonlit night can for one brief, exquisite moment bring back all of the enchantment that had once been theirs.

# *The Death Watch*

Hubert was dying. Imminently dying. In all likelihood he would not see another dawn. Greg, his sober and serious-minded lawyer son, knew this. Danny, his come-day, go-day, the-devil-take-Sunday-son, knew it. Tess, Hubert's one and only daughter-in-law, knew it. And certainly, Betsy, his wide-shouldered, strong-armed, indomitable wife of fifty years, knew it.

Indeed, just that morning she had admitted that for all the good her night of fervent and feverish praying had done her husband – for all the good her rosaries and litanies had done him – she might just as well have been beseeching the slop bucket beside his bed instead of the saints in heaven. If anything, Hubert's condition had worsened during the course of her praying. Early in the evening he had fallen into a heavy slumber, the kind of slumber that eventually gives way to death. By morning he had begun drowning in his own breath and the harsh, watery noises coming from his throat were unsettling everyone's nerves.

Betsy informed the family, along with Paddy Flynn, a neighbour who had come to help keep the death watch, that the strangling, watery noises coming from Hubert's throat was the Death Rattle. These rasping, burbling noises could be heard in every room in the house. They could be heard in the kitchen over the rolling boil of the water in the cast-iron kettle that Betsy had pulled to the front damper of the stove to make tea for supper. They could even be heard over the ferocious late spring storm that was scourging Hubert's wood-framed house and threatening to pry its window panes loose from their puttied moorings.

The five of them – Betsy, Greg, Danny, Tess, and Paddy – had gathered in the kitchen because it was suppertime and because it was the warmest room in the house. They sat around the table eating a fish chowder Tess had cobbled together in between making trips up to Hubert's room to check on him. Betsy looked as weather-beaten as the north-facing window casings, having spent the previous six weeks tending, mostly all on her own, to Hubert's needs. Now her sons tried to coax her to go to bed and to take one of the sleeping pills the doctor had left behind for her on his last visit to Hubert. She, however, had other plans.

"Let me alone!" she snapped crossly at Greg, who had been the more insistent of the two. "I'm not closing an eye until yer father reaches the other side. If I falls asleep, I can't depend upon any of ye to give him a Catholic death."

Danny broke in. "Hell, Mom, Dad's not even Catholic. You're the Catholic in this house. And what in the hell do you mean by a Catholic death? But if you'll go to bed, I'll see to it that he gets whatever kind of death ye wants."

He shrugged elaborately. "As far as I'm concerned death is death whether you're Catholic, Hutterite, or Dukhobor." Again he shrugged, this time with an accompanying impish grin. "But I might be wrong on that. I haven't died yet. Maybe they'll sling me up in a tree so the bears won't gnaw my bones."

"That's jest what I means," Betsy retorted, vindicated in her long-held belief that her lapsed Catholic son was unredeemable. "Ye spends yer life in the lumber woods in British Columbia and then comes home here to make smart remarks while yer poor father is at death's door. No respect for the dead and dying." She tossed her head scornfully. "But what more can ye expect from a backsliding Catholic."

Danny let the subject drop. He lit up a cigarette and concentrated on blowing perfectly round smoke rings into the air. He allowed a ring to soar almost all the way across the table before he reached up and poked his finger through it, breaking it open. In the wind from the leaky window casings, the smoke quickly disappeared.

"Danny's right, Mom," Greg hurriedly put in. "Lay out whatever it is you want done and we'll see to it that it's done. Rosaries, litanies – whatever you have in mind."

Paddy Flynn quickly sided with the brothers. "That's right, Mrs. Betsy. Ye needs yer rest. And I'll help them to look after things."

Betsy did not answer. She absently moved her spoon around in her chowder. After several minutes of silence, she said in a testing-the-waters sort of voice, "I bet if I was to go to sleep and that poor man was on the verge of dying, none of ye would put a lighted candle in his hand. Ye'd say that was a bunch of foolishness."

Her eyes quickly swept the table to take in the stunned expression on each face. Danny's mouth was wide open, aping exaggerated shock.

"Just like I thought," she said. "I knows ye all right. I knows ye to a T. So I'm stayin' up to do it meself."

"A lighted candle in his hand? What in the name of God are you talking about?" Danny asked, his tone incredulous. "That custom went out with Prince Albert tobacco. This is the 1980s."

Betsy held up her hand like a traffic cop. "Enough! Don't talk to me in that hoity-toity way. Me mother had a lighted candle. Me father had a lighted candle. Yer little sister Bridget had a lighted candle and yer father is going to get one, Catholic or not."

"What bloody foolishness is she going on with?" Danny asked, looking from Paddy to Greg to Tess and shaking his head in bafflement. "Ramming a flaming candle in Dad's hand! My God, that man's so weak he couldn't hold a fart, much less a flaming candle. What's she trying to do, cremate him?"

To diffuse Danny's outburst, Greg cut in quickly, his voice filled with deliberate reasonableness.

"Mom, that only disturbs the dying person. The Church knows that now. No one places a candle in a dying person's hand anymore. At least hardly anyone does. It interrupts the dying process. All that sort of stuff died out after Confederation."

"So sez you," Betsy scoffed, holding a plate loaded with thickly sliced homemade bread in Paddy's direction. "Well, I knows better. It's a comfort to the dying person. That's what 'tis. Ye places it in their hand the last moments before death. It's the last thing they sees on this earth – a blessed-by-the-Church candle lighting their way to heaven."

Paddy helped himself to a slice of bread. Betsy rearranged dishes on the table to make room for the bread plate. As she shuffled the dishes, she kept on talking about the candle that was ready and waiting for Hubert's dying hand.

"When I got the blessed candle on Candlemas Day, I put it aside for yer father. Even if the lights went out, I told meself I wouldn't use it. I'd keep it to light his way to heaven. Even back then I knew he was done fer."

Danny butted his cigarette in his saucer. A line of smoke quickly moved toward the leaky window casings as if it were a jet stream streaking across the sky. His eyes followed the smoke.

"A hell of a lot of good a candle will do him tonight," he said, gesturing outside at the spruce trees in the yard that were heaving in the wind. "In a gale like this, the thing would gutter out in less than a half-second. If Dad's going to light his way out of here, what he needs is a smudge pot – you know, those lights they use around construction work. Not even a northeast wind can douse those things."

Betsy pounded her fist on her knee and barked, "That's enough disrespect out of you, young man!"

With her right thumb she measured off a sliver of fingernail on her left thumb to show the minuscule amount of knowledge Danny had about his religion.

"Ye don't know *that* much about the religion you were baptized in. Not *that* much!"

Knowing that Danny would be quick to make a smart remark about the minuscule piece of thumbnail Betsy had just measured off, Greg gave him a cautioning look that said not to antagonize her any further or she'd never go to bed. Danny quickly changed his tactic. He lit up another cigarette and cupped it in his hand as he usually did, confining the smoke to the fleshy part of his thumb that was yellow from years of nicotine. He got up from his chair and squatted down at Betsy's knee.

"'Pon my soul, Mom," he said, crossing his heart with the hand that was cupping the cigarette, "I give you my word I'll do it for you. If you go to bed, I'll make sure that candle will be in Dad's hand at the last minute. I won't even wait until the last minute. I'll light up the bloody thing at least ten minutes before his last breath. I'll hold it in his hand myself. 'Pon my soul I won't let you down."

Betsy pulled herself up straight in her chair, fluffing herself up like a brooding hen.

"'Pon *yer* soul! My Jesus, Mary, and Joseph, b'y," she sneered. "Me depend upon *yer* soul! *Yer* word! Where in the name of the Holy Mother of God would that leave yer poor father? And I've got enough to account fer already with the two of ye giving up the Church, without trusting yer father's last breath to ye."

But his childish promise had apparently softened

her heart because after a few minutes she said, rising from her chair, "Yer right, me son. I needs me rest. I'll take me pill and go to bed. I'll leave the responsibility of yer father's candle with the three of ye."

She added as an extra precaution, "With the four of ye. You too, Paddy. I'll thank ye to make sure that Hube gets his candle."

The instant Danny heard the dull bang of Betsy's swollen bedroom door closing behind her, he began clearing up the supper dishes. Once everything was cleared away, he went into the pantry and came back out carrying a case of Black Horse beer in one hand and a bottle opener in the other. Paddy went to the porch and came back in also lugging a case of Black Horse – a case he had stashed out there on his way in, out of Betsy's sight. Both of them, each one clutching a case of beer, left the kitchen, along with Greg and Tess, to begin the death watch.

Upstairs, the storm seemed even worse than it had in the kitchen. It appeared to have gathered strength. Rain pelted hard on the flat, tarred roof and the house swayed on its rafters with each surge of wind that slammed up against the clapboards.

Hubert's sickroom – the smallest but nicest room in the house – had space only for one chair, so the four of them made camp in the narrow hall outside Hubert's door. A naked forty-watt bulb hung by a long cord from the ceiling and in this dim, yellow light, Greg tried to read material for an upcoming court case. Paddy and Danny began drinking immediately, offering a bottle to Greg and Tess as a courtesy even though they knew neither one of them drank beer. Both Danny and Paddy drank bottle after bottle and smoked cigarette after cigarette so that before long the air around them was fog-coloured and the wall that separated the hall from Hubert's bedroom was lined bumper to bumper with empty bottles.

In between the drinking and smoking they swapped jokes in an effort to block out the sound of the spine-chilling watery noises that were still escaping from Hubert's throat. As the beer disappeared and the night wore on, their jokes became raucous and their laughter got louder. From time to time, Greg had to shush them into silence.

After one particularly loud guffaw, Greg chastised, "Don't you fellows know hearing's the last faculty to go? How would you like to be lying in that bed dying and the rest of us out here laughing and joking?"

In their eagerness to apologize, their words tumbled over each other.

"Sorry, b'y! Sorry!"

"Sorry!"

For several minutes they remained silent. The silence magnified the sounds coming from Hubert's throat so unmercifully that Danny could not stand it any longer. He reached over and plucked at Greg's arm.

"Talk to us, Greg! Put those damn papers away and say something. Tell us some crooked lawyer stories. Or better yet, tell us about that lighted candle thing. You seemed to know something about it. Meself, I never heard of it before."

He gestured towards his mother's room. "She has the table all set up in Dad's room. Matches and candle and a candle holder. All ready for a seance or something."

Reluctantly, Greg allowed himself to be drawn into the conversation.

"Like she said, it's to light your way to heaven. An old Druid custom, I believe. Pagan. But I don't think anyone realized the origin of it. And for the most part it's been done away with. But I don't think Mom's been at a deathbed in thirty years so she still thinks that's the custom."

Greg returned to his reading. Paddy began nodding asleep, leaning against the wall. Danny stared at the grotesque shapes that the ceiling light was casting on the wallpaper as it swung back and forth with each gust of wind. Desperate to break the tension that was piling up inside of him, he jumped up and began singing, his words barely more than a whisper.

"'Twas on the Labrador me b'ys, 'twas on the Labrador." He scuffed around the floor doing a make-shift step-dance.

"Shut up, Danny!" Greg ordered. "Next thing you know you'll have Mom up tearing us all to shreds."

Danny retorted, "I don't give a shag if we wake up everyone in the Cove. I can't stand it any longer, listening to that poor bugger in there strangling himself to death."

He crouched down on the floor and picked up an empty bottle and scooted it across the linoleum floor towards Paddy, who was still lying back with his eyes closed and his mouth wide open. The bottle hit him on the foot.

"Come on, Paddy, me son. Wake up, b'y. Yer not here to get yer beauty sleep. Talk to me and Tess. Talk to Greg. Tell us some stories. Yer full of stories."

Paddy shuffled himself alert.

"Did I ever tell you about the time me mudder went to Boston to visit my sister and she died up there and they flew her body home to St. John's and my God Almighty they lost her?"

In unison Danny and Tess quickly said they hadn't heard the story. Greg, too, shook his head. By now even he was showing signs that he needed a distraction from Hubert's watery breathing because a few minutes earlier he had laid his reading material aside and had begun softly slapping his hands on his upper legs as if he were beating a drum. Paddy took a swallow of beer and wiped his mouth dry with the palm of his hand.

"Well, 'twas like this," he said, his voice already thick and fuzzy from the many bottles of Black Horse he had imbibed. "She had a heart attack and died and they sent her body home on the plane. My sister couldn't come with her because at that time she had so many youngsters she practically had to turn them outdoors in order to count them. So me and Bridey went to the airport to pick up Mudder and bring her back to our place."

Then, in case anyone present didn't know, he outlined the preparations that were needed to convert a parlour into a mortuary.

"We brought in the kitchen chairs to lay the coffin on. Four of them. Got out the candles." He motioned his thumb towards Hubert's room. "Jest like that candle in there. Very same pale yellow colour. Only we had two of them. Got them on Candlemas Day. Mopped and dusted and threw out the flies that had hung around the parlour over the winter. And we brought in lilacs. Hardly opened, mind you, even though it was mid-June. Caplin Scull time. Ye knows what that's like. Nothing but fog. On top of that we had the coldest damn spring. The harbour still had slob ice. There was even a bloody big iceberg ground-ed out there. It got too close to the shore and got hitched up in the shallow water. Just off the light-house. Got some neighbours to come stay with the children so me and Bridey and me brother-in-law, Thomas Kiervan, could go to the Torbay Airport.

"Didn't have a hearse out here either so I had to borrow a station wagon from Mick Riley up the road. Fer the coffin, ye see."

He stopped the telling and said as an aside, "You probably don't know this, Danny, you being away all the time, but we got a hearse here now." He nodded towards Tess. "Thanks to our MHA there. She wea-seled the money out of the government somehow. And a fellow from down the bay set up a funeral par-lour here that's every bit as good as the Newfound-land Hotel. 'Tis a damn shame ye have to be dead to overnight there. Anyway, back to me story."

Danny began to frantically flail his hands against his pockets, searching for matches. Finding none, he urgently interrupted, "Hold it! Hold it! Hold it right there! I'm out of matches."

He looked at Paddy. "You got matches, Paddy?"

"Naw, b'y, I've been usin' yers all night in case ye haven't noticed."

Danny remembered the packet of matches that Betsy had put in Hubert's room for lighting the can-dle. He went to get it. Within a few minutes he came back out, carrying the lighted candle in its holder, holding it aloft. Greg made a hurried motion to get up.

"Oh my God! Is it time? Is he going?"

"Naw, b'y. He's still breathing steady. There was only one match in the packet so I lit the candle. That way I have all the lights I'll need and the candle will be ready when the time comes."

Clutching the candle holder in one hand and his cigarette in the other, Danny gingerly lowered himself down on the floor. Once settled, he slipped the cigarette between his lips and bent low over the candle and drew flame into the tobacco. He straightened up, exhaled a mouthful of smoke, and laid the candle holder on the floor. With the back of his hand he carefully shunted it towards the wall, out of harm's way.

Paddy resumed his story.

"When I gets to the airport I goes up to the counter and asks fer Mudder. Two fellows there. In uniforms. There wasn't a passenger in sight. Not a soul. 'It's cleared out,' one of the fellows tells me, as if I can't see for meself. So I tells them I didn't expect to find her in the waiting room. She was in a coffin when she left Boston."

Paddy shook his head at the remembered flurry of action that followed this statement.

"My sonny b'y, as soon as I said that, their eyes darted to a sheet of paper they had laid out on the counter. Passenger list, I s'pose. Maybe it said Mudder's coffin was s'posed to be on the plane. Anyway, as soon as they scanned that paper, they took off."

He swiped his hands together. "Jest like that they took off! I could see them making phone calls.

They went out back to the freight shed. They came back in and made more phone calls. They looked in corners. Finally, they admitted – pretty sheepishly, mind you – that they had lost poor Mudder."

Paddy halted the telling long enough to uncap two fresh bottles of beer. He passed one to Danny. He took a few quick gulps from his own bottle and wiped his mouth dry with his sweater sleeve.

"'Blood of a bitch, buddies,' I sez, 'how could ye lose Mudder? Like I said, she was in a coffin. Nailed shut. No way she could wander off. Not like she could belly up to a bar and get plastered and miss the flight.'"

His tone suddenly changed, became more subdued. "And right away I started thinkin' of all those people back home in the parlour waitin' for her, the people Bridey notified before we left and the lilacs wiltin' in the water jugs, givin' off a dead smell even without a body. And I got thinkin' of the fire in the kitchen stove having to be kept low so the wake room wouldn't heat up, and of the house being filled with relatives and now we'd have to hold them over until we found Mudder. Even my Uncle Matt said he was goin' to try and make it to the house and he's so thin you can hear him cuttin' the wind when he walks by. Always sick he is. Most of the time 'tis jest to get attention. Enjoys poor health, ye might say."

He shrugged. "But he's me mudder's brother, so what else could I do?"

He returned once more to his main story.

"Another fellow in a uniform who said he heard me yellin' came out and told me another plane was comin' in and they were too busy to deal with me right then. He said for me to go back home and they'd get in touch with me later. Made it seem as if I was makin' a fuss over a lost suitcase or the like."

Paddy straightened up, wiped his mouth with the heel of his hand, removing droplets of beer. "Well, sir, that did it. 'Go back home without Mudder!' I sez, 'because yer too busy to find her!'"

Paddy slid across the linoleum floor so he was squashed up against Danny. "So I sidled right up to him so close like this, I could smell the fish cakes he had for breakfast and I said, 'Look here, buddy, I don't care if yer busier than a rooster with two dicks. I'm not leavin' here 'til ye finds me mudder.'"

Tess, Danny, and Greg burst into uproarious laughter. Greg even forgot to muffle his mouth. Paddy continued with his story as if unaware he had said something amusing. He pointed at Tess's blouse.

"I'm tellin' ye right now, he turned whiter than Tess's blouse. Whiter than the insides of a tuna fish. In fact, I've seen corpses with more of a flush."

Sensing he had gone on long enough, he took a swallow of beer and rounded up his story.

"So they made phone calls and made phone calls. And ran here and ran there. And between the jigs and the reels, the long and the short of it was they found poor Mudder out in Vancouver. Upended in a hangar. A fellow from here who works out there in that same hangar told me that when he came home for a visit. Said they had her leaning up against the wall like an old lobster pot against a shed."

Paddy took a deep, shuddering breath. "It was some bad feelin' when I heard that. I knows she was dead and all but to think ... But he could have been adding on. He's one to always make things worse than they are."

He broke off abruptly. Tears began streaming down his face and he used his sleeve to wipe them away. He fumbled with his beer bottle, wiping its neck with the heel of his hand.

Danny reached over and clapped him on the shoulder.

"I knew yer mother. Mrs. Agnes was a good woman. And those buggers treated her like an old dog. And that hurts. I know it hurts because ..."

Danny's voice suddenly choked. "Hell!" he blurted out. "Hell! I don't want Dad to die. I never really knew him. Left home when I was seventeen. We had words before I left home. Never told anyone. Never settled things between us. Now 'tis too late. Way too late."

Danny withdrew his hand from Paddy's shoulder and rubbed it over his own face in rapid strokes. In the half-light, the flaming ash of his cigarette looked as if there was a firefly crawling over him. "Hell!" he said again. "Hell!"

Greg reached out and awkwardly patted Danny's knee.

"That's all right, Danny boy," he said, his voice unusually gruff. "Seemed bad at the time, I s'pose, whatever it was. But he never said anything to me. Nor to Mom, for that matter, because I think she would have told me."

Danny kept his head bent, his eyes focused on his knees. "But he never believed me." His voice was little more than a whisper. "That's what hurts. Didn't want to believe me. If I was telling the truth, then that other blood of a bitch – Reverend Mose no less – would have to be shown up for what he was. A *diddler*. A child *diddler*. Everything would have to be brought out into the open. And Father didn't want a sniff of scandal to touch his church and give Mother fodder to make slights at the Anglicans whenever he ran down the Catholics. I'm certain that's why."

Greg sensed peril. He withdrew his hand from Danny's knee and sat bolt upright as if someone had punched him in the kidneys. Paddy and Tess sat up straighter as well.

"What are you getting at, Danny? What happened?" Greg asked, his voice bloated with foreboding.

"Nothing, b'y. Nothing at all," Danny said quickly and dismissively. He laid his cigarette on the neck of his beer bottle so he could use both hands to swab away the tears that he wanted to pretend were not there. He forced steadiness into his voice. "Just the beer talking. Just foolishness. Childish stuff. Forget it!"

"It's not foolishness if it hurt you that much," Greg insisted. He reached out and placed his hand back on Danny's knee. "Tell us what it was. Come on! Tell us!"

Danny jumped up, muttering he had to go downstairs to get more beer. In his hurry and clumsiness, he tipped over the candle everyone had forgotten about.

"Oh, hell's flames!" he sputtered, seeing the sea of congealing wax that had spread out over the linoleum floor. He hurriedly fumbled the small stub of candle upright. "Look what I've done. I've buggered Dad's candle. It's gone to nothing. Mom'll have me hide."

Greg, Paddy, and Tess rushed in to help, but all of their efforts only ended up in a humped-up mess of hardening wax.

Danny frantically turned to Tess. "Are there any more candles?"

Tess shook her head. "Just a red one I gave her for Christmas. But that won't do."

"We could shave off the red," Danny said, grasping at straws as he continued to uselessly mound the soft wax into a hump. "It might be white inside."

Tess shook her head again. "It's too big. As big as a tumbler. Never fit in Mr. Hube's hand."

Paddy whispered, his voice urgent, "Don't let the wick drown! A stub is better than nothing. You'll never get it relit if it drowns."

Greg grabbed a bottle cap and began bailing out the well of liquid that was threatening to snuff out the wick. He stopped suddenly, straightened up, and cocked an ear towards Hubert's room and hissed, "Listen! Listen!"

They listened. They heard the wind and the rain. They heard the rattle of the windowpanes. What they didn't hear was Hubert's breathing.

The four of them scrambled to their feet. Greg rushed to wake up his mother. Danny raced into his father's room. Tess grabbed the stub of candle out of its holder and held it cupped in her hand so as not to douse the flame. She hastily followed behind Danny. Paddy snatched up the candle holder and kept pace beside her. As he hurried, he shoved an empty cigarette packet underneath the candle in Tess's hand to save the dripping wax from scorching her flesh. Tess went to Hubert's side and picked up his cooling, lifeless hand and, after stuffing the candle stub back in its holder, she wrapped his hand around it because by this time there wasn't enough candle to hold onto all by itself. As soon as she had his hand secured in place, she looked at Paddy, who looked at Danny, who looked back at Tess. Each knew what the other was thinking: If Hubert had found his way to heaven, he had to have fumbled for it in the dark.

## Next Summer, God Willing

Sadie Fitzpatrick's arms are elbow deep in her bread-making pan as she pummels a mound of dough into submission. Up. Over. Down. Up. Over. Down. The old, uneven-bottomed aluminum pan see-saws with every thrust of Sadie's calloused hands. She will keep up this battering until the dough is soft and shiny and filled with air bubbles that will crack like pistol shots in her silent, dimly lit kitchen.

She is alone in the kitchen. Her two young-est daughters are in bed. Tomorrow is a school day. Her only son is away working on the American base that had been built on the outskirts of Caplin Scull shortly after the beginning of World War ll. Her old-est child, Kathleen, had married a serviceman who had been stationed on that base. In fact Kathleen had done much the same as she, herself, had done – one war removed. She had married Alfred in 1915. At that time he was a member of the Newfoundland

Regiment and had come to Tralee on leave. Kathleen is now living in Virginia and she has a houseful of children. She always writes that she is going to come home, next summer, God willing, but Sadie knows those words spring from wishful thinking only. Her husband is like Alfred, who at this moment is lying on the parlour couch, sleeping off a binge of home-made beer.

Sadie looks much older than her years. A life of hardship is chiselled into her face. Her frame is raw-boned and her shoulders are rounded. When she is especially weary, or especially sad, her mouth droops. On this evening her mouth droops severely. The black-bordered telegram from Tralee that had arrived in the afternoon, while she was out cleaning the soot and cobwebs from Mary Lundergan's ceilings, is lying on the window ledge, soaking up the moisture from the leaky window casing. Sadie no longer needs to read the message. She knows it by heart. *Regret to inform you Mother passed away this afternoon ...*

She finishes pummelling the bread, pulls a table-cloth over the pan, and places it beside the stove so the heat will help the bread rise to at least double in size. Ordinarily, as was the custom in her home back in Tralee, the last thing a bread-maker would do before turning away from the bread pan would be to slice the sign of the cross over the pan, leaving its rising or falling to the mercy of God. This evening she does not swipe the sign of the cross over the bread pan, not caring whether the dough rises or falls, and not certain God will take any hand, act, or part in its rising or falling anyway.

Since the arrival of the telegram, she has lost all

hope of the Deity coming to her aid for something as mundane as bread rising. Or for anything else for that matter. She had been entreating Him for years to allow her to go back to Tralee to see her mother. Just one trip was all she had asked for. And He had ignored her request. And now it was too late. And besides, now that she had no reason to go back to Tralee, she no longer had an excuse for cleaning other people's dirt. The children had not been embarrassed by her going outside her house to work because it had been for a special purpose. But now the water-soaked envelope meant that the purpose had been taken away.

She unties her apron and tosses it on a chair and heads up to her bedroom. Hanging on a wall, at the head of her bed, is a wooden crucifix with a silver Christ suspended on it. She stands before the cross, but instead of her usual begging for a miracle, either big or small – such as making Alfred give up spending his war pension on hop beer, shell shock or no shell shock – she berates the silver Christ.

"Now You've really put me in a spot. What reason am I going to give the children for going out day after day to clean other people's houses? They're ashamed to have to say that their mother has to do cleaning work for the neighbours just to make ends meet. Saving to go to Tralee had been acceptable to them."

She turns away from the crucifix and walks out into the hall and begins to pace the floor. She flings words over her shoulder. "Maybe You don't even exist. Fer all I knows religion is jest a money racket."

She holds up the Mission Fathers as an example

of people who take money in the name of God. They had recently come from Detroit to do a mission in Caplin Scull. According to reports, they hadn't left a sin nor a cent in the village. She had gone to Confession to one of them and had mentioned about Alfred being no good since the war, hoping he would at least feel sorry for her. She had whispered through the grating, "Fadder, I know 'tis not right to talk bad about people, but between you and me, Alfred's no bloody good." In return she got a lecture on being uncharitable and three Hail Marys for penance.

Her thoughts flit from the Mission Fathers to her daughter, Kathleen, who is never far from her thoughts. In her mother's heart, she surmises that Kathleen has married a shiftless, no-good American soldier just like her own father, Alfred. Different war. Different country. Same quality of man. She continued to end her letters in the familiar litany, "I'm coming home. Next summer, God willing." But God never seemed to be willing to help her either. Every year she had another child – another mouth to feed.

Suddenly Sadie stops pacing. A thought slices through her brain with as much force as the bolt of lightning that had felled Paul from his horse on the road to Damascus. Indeed, she had to go in to her bedroom and sit down on her bed to keep from falling to her knees. *Her children would not have to be ashamed that she was a washerwoman who needed outside money to keep food on the table.* She would tell them another story. A different story. She would tell them that she was working to get extra money to bring Kathleen home for a visit. She was certain that would be acceptable to them.

In gratitude she looks up at the silver Christ on the wooden crucifix. "Thank You! Thank You!" she whispers reverently. She would simply say that although she no longer had a need to go back to Tralee, she had a daughter in Virginia who was homesick for Caplin Scull.

She will say to anyone who asks when Kathleen is going to be coming home, "Not this summer. Next summer, God willing."

# St. Patrick's School

St. Patrick, Ireland's patron saint, had been selected to be the patron saint of the one-room school in Caplin Scull. He was a fitting choice in that the eighteen or twenty students – the number fluctuating from month to month and year to year and ranging in age from five to sixteen – were all of Irish descent. You only had to hear the teacher call roll each morning to confirm this ancestry: Hennessey, Heffern, Whalen, Dooley, Fitzgerald, Callaghan, Corrigan, and Cochrane.

To ensure that the students were fully aware that St. Patrick was their benefactor, *their shelter from the stormy blast*, a large statue of him occupied the corner to the left-hand side of the teacher's desk. His graven image was resplendent in a green robe with gold trimming. A gold-coloured mitre covered his balding head, the mitre signifying that he was a bishop and in high standing with both God and man.

In his left hand he gripped a tall, substantial-looking staff which we believed was what he must have used to kill those snakes, the lifeless body of one such creature lying just inches from his sandalled feet.

With such power, such might, and such courage at the ready, how could the occupants of St. Patrick's school be other than successful? All that was needed to ensure our soaring to greatness both in this world and in the next was a bended knee and a sincere invocation: *Oh holy St. Patrick, protect us in our time of need!*

There were many occasions when both students and teacher were in dire need of St. Patrick's intercession. There were equally a number of times when our invocation appeared to have fallen on deaf ears. I am certain that our teacher must have beseeched him on that day when sixteen-year-old Cyril snatched the hardwood chalkboard pointer out of her hand and rammed it into her neck.

When I was in grade three, I won a prize for being the best-behaved student in the class. Even at the time of presentation, I was ashamed of that prize. I knew I had gotten it under false pretenses. It was fear, not virtue, that had made me the quietest in the room. I was eight and my desk was at the front. Ernest sat directly behind me. Ernest, too, was sixteen and big for his age. He was also sadistic. Once he tied two cats together and threw them over the electric wires between poles and watched with delight as they tore each other to death.

What Ernest hated even worse than cats was for anyone in front of him to squirm or talk. Every time

I moved or spoke, he would get out his box of Eddy's safety-tipped matches and singe my hair. It became a Hobson's choice for me: be quiet and have a full head of hair when the school closed in June or squirm and be totally bald by then. I winged many a prayer to St. Patrick asking that he have some tragedy befall Ernest, but apparently all of my invocations went unheeded because month after month Ernest continued to remain robust and healthy and viciously cruel.

Henry Corrigan was another student who could have used a little help from St. Patrick. Henry was in grade two when I was in grade two. He was still in grade two when I was in grade five. Henry snarled up the alphabet. To him, W's looked like M's, P's were upside-down d's. An S was just a squiggle that could be turned backwards or forwards. He also was unable to distinguish between a long vowel and a short vowel sound. Not surprisingly he never learned to read. However, he could make sweet music whenever he would place a cigarette paper over the teeth of a comb and use it as a makeshift harmonica. He also fashioned whistles out of willow saplings. Once he built a fiddle out of rabbit wire, strips of cardboard, oilcloth, and the remnants of a discarded accordion.

Henry dropped out of school at thirteen. He was labelled an idler and it was believed that his laziness would be better served by helping his father spread manure on the hay meadows. He left school in late spring. He left the village soon afterward. He left even before the aroma from his father's meadows could crawl in through the cracks in the school's windows. No one appeared to know his destination, nor did they concern themselves about it.

I have often wondered whether St. Patrick could have helped Henry become a famous maker of fiddles if he had taken him under his staff, so to speak.

And there was Martha. It was generally understood that Martha "had a room or two upstairs not finished." What was not understood was the need for our charity. Martha spelled words by using a mixture of sounds and letters. Mug, for example, was spelled *mu-egg*. Jacket pocket was spelled *ja-ecket po-ocket*. Her spelling attempts were always the most enjoyable parts of the school day.

And then there was Aloysious. Aloysious was often punished for not completing his homework assignment. The teacher had no idea that Aloysious' cruel stepfather would not let him do his homework because he got great joy out of hearing that his stepson had been punished for his homework negligence.

I have often wondered whether anyone had acquainted St. Patrick with the fact that he was our benefactor and as such was supposed to be our help in all adversities. I have also wondered whether he had ever been asked by anyone for help and he had ignored the implorer. Certainly any man who could squash snakes with his bare feet could have found a way to help those in desperate need. The least he could have done was persuade a benefactor, or the Church for that matter, to donate enough money to keep the pot-bellied stove in lengths of wood for five hours a day so that we did not have to write while wearing our homespun mitts. And was there anything that he could have done for or about Ernest? The last anyone heard of him he was in jail in St. John's. For arson. The people in the village pronounced it *arsing* and said they weren't at all surprised that he had run afoul of the law. I took the news to mean that he had found a more exciting use for his safety-tipped matches other than singeing hair.

# *Stranded*

That's right. The son of a bitch left me stranded at the altar. At a side altar I hasten to say. If you were in the family way, you couldn't be married at the main one. There were two side altars in our church – the main one was in between them. St. Joseph's altar was on the right-hand side and Holy Mother's was on the left. If you were in the family way, you were made to stand at Holy Mother's.

A slap in the face to the Holy Mother, I'd say. Anyone who wasn't pure enough for the main altar would be quietly and without fanfare shuffled off to her altar to be united in matrimony, not necessarily holy matrimony. The clergy didn't want an unchaste woman parading in front of St. Joseph, but with Mary, a woman who was inviolate from the beginning to the end, it was a whole other thing. Way beyond my understanding. A man-made rule for sure. Of course, it may have been that I've sized it up all wrong. It may have been that since it was the woman who chose the altar, it was because she felt the Virgin Mary would be more understanding and compassionate.

I was four months along when I stood at the altar and if I had had any say in the matter, or any sense in my head for that matter, I would never have owned up to being in the family way. As soon as Father found out he went to Father Henley to put pressure on the groom to marry me and, of course, once my predicament was brought out in the open, I lost all hope of the main altar.

On the day of my wedding, the church was as cold as the grave. It was early November and the dress I was wearing had been made of flimsy material and had three-quarter-length sleeves. Mother bought the dress from a peddler. Back then there was no way I could get into St. John's to buy one from the Water Street stores – not that I had the money to do that anyway. I would have had to go by train to St. John's and stay overnight. In 1938 – the tail end of the Great Depression years in Newfoundland – there was no money in the coffers for that sort of luxury.

I was nineteen at the time and I had never worked a day in my life outside of my father's house. But God knows I had worked hard enough inside it. I was gutting codfish. Or spreading caplin out to dry. Or planting potatoes. Or washing floors. Or shearing sheep. I could go on and on. All unpaid, of course, excepting for free food and a roof over me head.

Peddlers used to come out on the train from St. John's with large suitcases stuffed mostly with clothes, but they also carried cure-all ointments and backache pills. Every pantry was stockpiled with Carter's Little Liver Pills. The peddlers would lug those suitcases door to door. The dress Mother bought for me was way too big but when she altered it, it certainly hid my condition. Years later I came upon the same colour of dress in Eaton's catalogue. It was called "electric blue." A bilious colour then and a bilious colour now. But what choice did I have? A neighbour loaned me a hat. It was too big for me as well, but hat pins held it on. Borrowed my mother's Sunday shoes because my own were scuffed at the heels. Had to stuff paper into the toes to make them fit so I could hobble down the aisle.

It was a cold, wet November day and there was only a handful of people in the church, although the whole village was welcome to attend the ceremony. As well, they were welcome to come back to our house afterward for a feed of bully beef and freshly baked bread and molasses muffins. The few who said they were coming were direct neighbours who could easily walk to our house.

Those same neighbours, along with the groom's sister and brother-in-law, were already in the church by the time I got there. His parents had died several years earlier. My father had harnessed up our horse to our Sunday carriage. My maid of honour rode with us. The best man was waiting at the church, along with a couple of stragglers I barely knew, but they were the kind who would attend a witch burning if it meant getting free food afterwards. Other than those few, the church was empty.

We waited for the groom to arrive. I was trembling head to toe. But not just from the cold. Some sixth sense in the pit of my gut told me he wasn't going to show up. The best man said he had stopped by his house to pick him up on his way to the church, but he had found no one at home. He just assumed that someone else must have brought him to the church.

Only three people in the village had telephones and the best man wasn't one of them or he would have telephoned the groom before he left his own house. The priest had a telephone. So did the post-mistress and so did Kevin Walsh, the owner of the general store. After an embarrassing wait, Father Henley got in touch with Kevin Walsh and asked him to try to get in touch with the groom by one means or another. If you needed any information about the goings-on in the village, you got in touch with Kevin. In a manner of speaking, the world passed through his store every day and anything that happened without his knowledge wasn't worth knowing about.

Kevin reported that he saw "Himself" heading for the train station about an hour earlier that morning. He was walking at the time and carrying a suitcase. The train came out from St. John's three times a week. Unloaded freight and passengers, then up-loaded freight and passengers before turning around and heading back to St. John's. Kevin's fleeting thought at that time was that maybe he was meeting someone at the station – someone who was coming out from St. John's for the wedding. But the suitcase made no sense, although it made sense later on once he got the call from the priest.

Oh, the shame of it all. Especially for Mother and Father. Although they hadn't jumped for joy over my choice of husband, they certainly hadn't expected things to turn out the way they did. But I must give the people in Caplin Scull their due, because no matter how much they may have chewed on what had happened behind closed doors, they offered us genuine sympathy to our faces. Some even shed a tear when I went to their home to return the wedding gifts. Nearly everyone said, "What goes around comes around." I always forced a smile and said, "For sure it does," but even back then I knew that saying rarely holds true. Some gets what's coming to them. Some don't.

And then I lost the baby. Too much heartache, the doctor said. That was the final of a thousand cuts. There were those who said it was a blessing, but I felt as if I had been felled by an axe twice within a few weeks. All emotions left me for a very long time – anger, love, hate. I just plodded on, each day putting one foot in front of the other.

Then World War II started up. The Americans came and built a base not far from here. I got a job in one of their laundries. Worked there for four years. After I got a bit of money saved, I went to the General Hospital in St. John's and trained to be a ward aid. A good steady and respectable job that didn't depend on a war. Met a couple of men who would have liked to marry me. But I was never again going to stand in front of an altar and wait for a man to not show up. Perhaps I shortchanged myself, but I've never regretted staying single.

He never penned a note to say he was sorry or to explain why he had done what he had done. I heard via others that he had gotten a job in a factory that made zippers. In those days it wasn't hard to hear news from Boston. Everyone in these parts had a son or daughter or brother or sister in Boston. They all would gang together up there on Sundays and share news from home.

The only times I've thought of him over the years have been whenever I've gotten a zipper stuck. I'd say under my breath, "Goddamn you, Michael Hartigan, ye were always a foul-up. Can't even make a zipper that works."

Now whatever possessed me to get started on this subject today? The long and the short of it is, we've all got crosses to bear and Michael Hartigan has been mine to sling over my shoulder and keep on walking. Actually, I'm proud of the way I carried the load.

# The Devil is a Gentleman

Sarah Heffrin was agitated almost to the point of being frantic. Too late she realized she had not only underestimated her father's abhorrence for the evils of dancing, but she had overestimated her ability to wheedle him into capitulating to her request.

It was Saturday evening and the dance at the Star of the Sea hall, sponsored by the Roman Catholic Church in the town, would soon be starting. She had counted on being able to persuade her father, the newly arrived magistrate to the tiny outport town on Newfoundland's east coast, to let her go to the dance if she promised merely to sit and watch.

But he had been adamant in his refusal. It was bad enough, he said, that she, being Protestant, had to attend a Catholic school, without also participating in the sinful social life of dancing and card playing that the Romans indulged in.

Sarah wished she had owned up to the truth on

Friday before she left the school. She wished she had told her classmates she would not be attending the dance. She wished she had admitted to them that her father considered dancing to be the gyrations of the devil and whenever this behaviour spilled over into the Sabbath it was sinful in the extreme.

Her face burned in anticipation of the humiliation she was certain to experience when she went to school on Monday morning and had to admit she had lied about going to the dance, and that her religion forbade dancing. Already she could hear the whispers and giggles. And they would not even have the decency to wait until she was out of earshot.

The more she contemplated what awaited her at that convent schoolhouse on Monday morning, the more severe her anticipated humiliation became. Mortification filled every crease and crevice of her body, every nook and cranny of it. Around six o'clock that evening, when she could no longer bear up under the pain, she tossed aside the commandment Honour Thy Father and Thy Mother, and stormed into her father's musty-smelling study and snapped a command at him.

"Give me one good reason, Father, why I can't go to that dance!" Her eyes blazed with indignation. "Everyone in my class is going. I'll be the laughingstock of the school."

She hotly repeated, "*One good reason*. That's all I ask." On the surmise he would offer her a Biblical quotation with no relevance for the present-day, she added scornfully, "I mean one *sound* reason. Not some reason that was pulled out of some stone-age reading."

She had found him sitting at his desk, squinting in the glare of a kerosene lamp trying to decipher yellowed handwritten pages of court documents that were so old the pages were as brittle as rice paper. He had ignored her rudeness in not knocking and pretended not to hear her command. He was far too weary to strike up yet another quarrel with his daughter.

"Father!"

When he didn't answer her immediately, she prodded, "One sound reason. That's all I'm asking."

Without taking his eyes from the papers spread out before him, he quoted softly, "*I have not brought ostracism upon Israel, but you and the house of your father have done so because you men have left the commandments of God and you went following the Ba'als.*"

As a rule, Sarah always bowed her head whenever her father quoted from Scripture, but now she was far too distressed to concern herself with propriety and circumstance.

"Oh, for mercy sakes," she cut in disgustedly. "You're talking about demonic dances again. Can't you understand this is nineteen and thirty – not *Elijah's Era!*"

Once more Magistrate Heffrin let his daughter's insolence slide by without reprimand. He sighed heavily, and Sarah, mistaking his sigh for the onset of capitulation, softened her attack.

"Please, Father," she implored, her voice tender and wheedling. "I promise to leave before midnight. And I promise not to dance. I just want to be seen there so I won't get mocked when I go to school on Monday."

He looked up from his papers, and quoted once more, his voice calm, his words firm: *"Can a man take fire in his bosom and his clothes not be burned?"*

In that defining quotation, Sarah realized defeat. She could feel the pain of her exclusion on Monday morning. She was certain that death would be less terrible and she hoped her demise would come before the weekend was over.

With nothing to lose and apparently nothing to gain, she lashed out one more time, using the profanity she had heard outside her home.

"For God's sake, Father. Is that the best you can do? Quote outdated Scripture? No wonder we're the laughingstock of this whole town."

Magistrate Heffrin sprang from his chair with such force he created a draft that sent tongues of smoke-edged flame up the lamp chimney.

"Never! Never! Never!" he commanded, wagging his finger within inches of Sarah's face. "Never while you are under my roof are you to let me hear you profane the Lord's name again!"

His jowls above his starched white collar trembled with righteous indignation. "And as for dancing ..." Here he paused to let the foul taste of the word clear his tongue. "Don't you ever utter that evil word in this house again!"

Sarah didn't wait to be excused. She raced from the room, but not before her father caught sight of the hatred and contempt that contorted her face.

\* \* \* \* \*

Magistrate Heffrin sank back down in his chair, spent and exhausted. He leaned on his elbows and tried to knuckle the harsh lamplight out of his eyes. He wished he had never come to this town, miles away from St. John's. It had been a mistake to accept a job in a community where everyone else belonged to a religion that was so foreign to his own beliefs.

But he had wanted to make a new start, hoping it would help him get over his wife's recent death. However, the irony was that it had only served to make him miss Margaret's presence even more. And he had to accept the fact that on account of his own selfish need, Sarah was now turning into a godless creature. She was mixing with young people who saw nothing wrong with dancing or card playing or even games of chance. Even on the Sabbath! He had heard that every time the Romans held a church bazaar, there was a wheel of fortune on hand encouraging even the children to gamble away their nickels and pennies. And they excused these games of chance by saying the proceeds from them went for the upkeep on their church. But even worse than the games of chance, even worse than the card playing, was their practice of dancing on the Sabbath!

His heart bled for his daughter. It bled even while he was severely chastising her. She had lost both her mother and her school friends all within the space of a year and in the town to which he had brought her, she felt as alien as Ruth in the land of Naomi.

"If only Margaret had lived," he sighed and then left the thought incomplete, just as his life had been left incomplete with her death.

He slowly rose to his feet and picked up the lamp and left his cluttered office. He was bone weary. He was weary of living in a community that had too little of everything. There wasn't even enough crime to keep him in the courthouse for more than a few hours a month. He was weary of arguing with Sarah. Most of all, he was weary of loneliness.

Before ascending the stairs to his bedroom, he called softly in the direction of the kitchen.

"I'm going to bed, Sarah. Don't stay up too long because it's a cold night out even for December and you'll get chilled once the fire burns down."

Sarah didn't answer. She continued to stare sullenly into the dying embers of the spruce logs. To save on fuel costs they never kept the fire going after the evening meal was cleared away. She shivered and drew her homespun shawl closer around her shoulders. But the chill she felt had nothing to do with the kitchen fire. It was hopelessness that was causing her temperature to drop. Any expectation she may have had about her father relenting and letting her go to the dance had vanished when she heard his footsteps climbing the stairs.

She went over to the window and with her fingernail scraped the frost from one of the narrow panes of glass. The peephole gave her a view of the Star of the Sea hall. Lanterns flickered and blinked from the stomping of the dancers doing the quadrille. She heaved with her shoulders against the window frame to push it open so she could hear the accordion music through the narrow crack. A wildly wicked thought entered her mind. *What if I went to the hall and didn't let Father know? What he doesn't know won't hurt him. And if I don't dance, I can't see how I would be committing any sin at all.*

She tried to banish the temptation from her mind by slamming the window shut and going back to sit beside the stove. She berated herself for having had such an evil thought. Certainly, she would never disobey her father and sneak out of the house!

She could still faintly hear the accordion music even with the window shut. She got up to go to bed. She decided she would open the window again for just a moment before heading up the stairs. This time the lanterns didn't just flicker. They winked. They taunted. They beckoned. The music mocked her earth-locked feet. It tantalizingly called her name.

*Diddle dee, diddle dee. Diddle dee, diddle dom.*
*Sarah Heffrin, won't you come.*

She shut the window once more and crept up the stairs to change into her Sunday dress, reiterating her promise to herself that she would not dance. Not even one step. Not that she knew how to dance any steps. She wouldn't even permit herself to sway to the music. And certainly she would be home before midnight. She would never allow herself to be in a dancehall on the Sabbath.

Just before she left the house she went to the cupboard and dipped her hand into the brown earthenware crock that held the housekeeping money. She took only enough for her admission ticket. She then tiptoed across the kitchen floor and eased the outside door ajar, closing it softly behind her. She breathed easily when she heard the night latch fall securely into place.

\* \* \* \* \*

They were just choosing partners for a set of waltz numbers when she entered the hall. Several young men invited her to dance but she politely refused, insisting she wanted only to watch. She sat by the wall and stared mesmerized as the dancers looped and swirled across the rough wooden floor. She was so intent on watching the dancers that she didn't notice a young man approach her.

"Oh, I didn't mean to startle you, miss," he apologized quickly when he saw her wide-eyed taken-off-guard look. "I just wanted to have this dance with you."

Flustered, she stammered, "I ... No ... I mean, I don't dance ... I mean, I can't dance." She was about to say, I'm not allowed to dance, but he forestalled her.

"Certainly you can dance," he easily assured her. "Besides, I'll not accept refusal from the prettiest girl in the room."

He smiled broadly, showing white, even teeth. Sarah was certain he had to be the most handsome man in the world. In his black suit and starched white shirt he resembled an Arabian prince.

She shook her head and dropped her gaze to the floor. She could feel a blush leaving her neck and moving up to her cheeks. She wished the young man would go away and stop embarrassing her, while at the same time she wished he would stay close to her forever.

"Come on," he coaxed. "I'll teach you how to waltz. There's really nothing to it. See?" *One, two three. One, two three.* He danced in front of her as gracefully as a ballerina.

Even in her confusion she was conscious of the fact that if she danced with this handsome fellow, all of the girls would envy her. They might even stop thinking of her as being odd and different. She wondered if just one dance would break her promise to herself, especially if to make up for dancing the one dance she would leave the hall immediately afterwards.

The young man saw her resolve begin to weaken and he pressed his advantage. He extended his hand and said, "My name's Peter. Peter Bradshaw. I'm a stranger in these parts." His voice teased. "You wouldn't be so uncharitable as to refuse a lonely stranger a dance, would you?"

She pulled her gaze from the floor and looked full into his face. She imagined his arms closing around her.

"Just one dance," she said demurely. "Just one dance and then I have to leave."

The instant she stepped upon the dance floor she forgot she had never danced before. With Peter guiding her, she felt as though her feet had been practising the steps for years. She forgot about her promise to leave before midnight. The music coursed through her body and made her oblivious to everything but the pressure of Peter's arms. She danced a second, a third, a fourth, and a fifth dance. Finally, she lost count. There was just her and Peter and the music.

"The last dance, ladies and gentlemen," the accordion player announced.

Sarah stiffened ramrod straight. Her feet stuck to the floor. *It couldn't be the last dance!* The evening had just begun! She looked out towards the windows. It was almost dawn!

She bolted from the hall, not even taking the time to tell Peter she was leaving. He saw her go and ran after her, insisting he walk her home. Nor did she take time to protest his offer but continued to race over the snow-packed gravel road, the magic of the evening disappearing in the grey light of dawn and in the awareness of the enormity of her disobedience and deception.

She had even committed sins of the flesh because she had longed to kiss the red circle on Peter's neck where the flesh had been rubbed raw from his heavily starched collar.

"Whoa, Sarah!" Peter shouted, as he tried to catch up with her. "Slow down!"

She slowed down only long enough to look over her shoulder. Peter Bradshaw's whole countenance had changed. It now terrified her. Even from the distance, she was certain she was looking upon evil. A chill ran up her spine. The crisp December air suddenly turned sodden and heavy.

"Go back!" she screamed. "Go back!"

She kept on running to get to the safety of her house. She raced up her porch steps, not even caring whether her father heard her or not. It only mattered that she get away from *Him* – the Antichrist she had been warned about.

She tried to open the door, but the knob wouldn't turn. Then she remembered she had closed the door without disengaging the night latch. And she hadn't brought her key.

She pounded on the door, screaming to her father to wake up. But she couldn't rouse him. She tried to find stones to pelt at his window, but they were all frozen to the ground and she couldn't pry them loose. Every now and again she stiffened with fear, certain she heard the latch on the garden gate opening and shutting, fearful that despite her admonishment Peter had continued to follow her. Her heart almost pounded out of her breast. Her breath caught in her throat. She fell into a heap at the bottom of the porch steps.

Her father found her later on that morning. She was insensible and in her delirium she kept mumbling what seemed to be passages from the Bible, but her speech was so indistinct that it was little more than a babble.

She lived for almost two weeks. The doctor said the frost had affected her lungs. And it had affected her brain as well, which explained her almost incomprehensible raving about the Devil, the Apostle of Darkness, who wanders this earth. Just before she drew her last breath, she sat bolt upright in bed and, with eyes glazed from the approach of imminent death, searched the room for her father.

"Father! Father!" she entreated, clearly and distinctly. *"Be sober, be vigilant because your adversary the devil as a roaring lion walketh about seeking whom he may devour."*

\* \* \* \* \*

Sarah's body was taken to St. John's for burial, but on the following day Magistrate Heffrin held open house for the people of the town to come and pay their respects. One of the men who came asked him about the young man that he had been told had followed Sarah out of the hall.

"His name is Bradshaw," the magistrate said. "Peter Bradshaw. He came to see me right after her funeral. A fine young man. He regretted having listened to Sarah when she told him to stop following her. He said she should never have left the hall without him. He said he's from out the shore. I told him that anytime he comes this way to come stay with me. Plenty of spare rooms in this house. That's for sure."

"Peter Bradshaw," the visitor repeated, his tone a question mark. "That name certainly sounds familiar." He squinted his eyes as his mind went back over time. "There used to be a family of Bradshaws here a long time ago. They lived out along the shore. But they've been dead for years. And good riddance! A father and a son, I believe. They were a devilish lot. Used to lure ships aground by removing the light from the channel shoal and when the ships smashed upon the rocks, they would go aboard and kill and plunder."

The man shook his head, recalling for the magistrate the many gruesome stories that had circulated in the town about the Bradshaws.

He ended hopefully, "But they got what was coming to them. A piece of rope ended their carnage. Both of them were hung in St. John's on the same day. And they died as flint-hearted as they lived. Or at least so it was said. I can't imagine Sarah's young man being related to those Bradshaws! And as you say, you took him to be a real gentleman."

# The Million

The news swept through Caplin Scull like a summer fire through the blueberry barrens that rimmed the village. Although Caplin Scull had only two telephones – one in the post office and the other in the Catholic rectory – within the space of a day or two, most, if not all, of the villagers had heard of the imminent windfall that would soon be coming their way. This was ecstatic news indeed, especially so for a community that was still trudging through the tag end of the Great Depression.

It all began when someone from Caplin Scull went into St. John's, the capital city, about a hundred miles away, and while in there he picked up a copy of the *Daily News,* the island's newspaper. A tiny column on the back page caught his eye. It was a notice from a lawyer in Boston who was searching for eligible heirs to a million dollars that had been left by a man named Morrissey – a lifelong resident of Boston who had died intestate. The connection with Caplin Scull was tenuous. Morrissey's ancestors hailed from County Cork in Ireland, as did the ancestors of the Morrisseys who had settled in Caplin Scull.

Apparently, this search for legitimate heirs to Morrissey's fortune had been ongoing for several years. In fact, it had been going on so long that the "dormancy period" was fast approaching. This article had explained that the dormancy period was a duration of time that had been allowed by the State of Massachusetts to find an heir to this money or otherwise it would revert to the State. Also, according to the article, the search for heirs had now been narrowed down to Caplin Scull, a tiny sea-battered village on the east coast of Newfoundland.

Almost a hundred percent of the inhabitants of Caplin Scull had some connection to the name of Morrissey. They were connected either through birth, marriage, or some other entanglement, so that even after sorting through the intermarriages of first cousins, double first cousins, second cousins once removed, and double second cousins, it became evident that almost every family in the community was bound to benefit in some way.

The year was 1938 – a time when the majority of the inhabitants of Caplin Scull were still living on a government handout called the dole. This handout amounted to the kingly sum of thirty-five cents per head of household per day. The month was March, known in the community as the hungry month of March because by this time of the year, winter supplies had dwindled but it was still too early for the inshore fishing industry to begin or road construction to get underway. Under such circumstances, it was quite understandable why the prospect of sharing in a million dollars was heady news for all concerned.

The few inhabitants of Caplin Scull who did not share blood ties or marriage ties with the Morrisseys began to manufacture such ties. Bobby O'Dearin, for example, who had been taken out of an orphanage in St. John's when he was seven and had been given a home with Bill and Lill Morrissey, believed he had a claim to the money. He maintained that because Bill and Lill had left him their parcel of hardscrabble land after their death, it would be only natural for them to leave him their share of any upcoming inheritance. He also pointed out that because Bill and Lill had been double first cousins, such close blood ties would certainly have entitled them to a twofold share of the windfall.

Mary Flannigan surprised everyone by stepping forward to claim her out-of-wedlock son's rightful share on his father's side even though his proclaimed father had never acknowledged him as his son. Scabs were pulled off scars that had taken years to heal. And to hide! As the story went, Mary had been paid handsomely to keep her mouth shut. She was now willing and eager to testify that yes, Little Ronnie Morrissey, the scalawag son of landowner Big Ron Morrissey, was the father of her child.

In the many cases where first cousins were married to second cousins, or where first cousins were married to each other, different squabbles arose. Having two heirs in one family was viewed by many as being tantamount to receiving twice as much as other families. It was, therefore, strongly put forward that each household should receive one share only, regardless of how many in that household were entitled to inherit. This stance was strongly vetoed by those who had more than one entitled person in their family.

Sarah Morrissey Fitzgerald, who had spent many years in an abusive marriage to Paddy Fitzgerald, viewed the inheritance as God's answer to her months and years of saying decades of her rosary and beseeching the Almighty to send help for Paddy's drinking problem. But making a teetotaller out of Paddy was even more than God could handle, so she had begun to pray for a short and painless death for Paddy. Now she brazenly announced that the very moment she would come into the money, she was going to turn tail and leave the fist-swinging Paddy to deal with his own vices. She vowed that the lips that touched liquor would never again touch hers.

Paddy, seeing the million slipping out of his reach, instantly sobered up. He immediately "took the pledge" in front of the "Consecrated Host" in the tabernacle on the altar of the Sacred Heart Church, vowing lifelong sobriety. However, it was said that at the time of his vow-taking he was so full of hop beer that he fell down the altar steps.

Willie Fagan fessed up that the often-surmised incestuous relationship between his mother and his grandfather was true. "Me aunt had me," he said. "That's the God's honest truth. Me aunt was me mother. Me grandfather was me father. There was no Portuguese sailor. They just said that to cover up." Because of this special familial relationship, he believed he should get a double share – his aunt's/mother's share along with his grandfather's/father's share.

At least one romantic relationship was smothered as quickly as it had burst into flame. A girl by the name of Philomena, whose mother was a Morrissey, was suddenly being fiercely courted by a man named Albert. Albert was one of the few in the village who had no relationship either through birth, marriage, or adoption to a Morrissey. Ever the opportunist, Albert began courting Philomena, although heretofore he would have considered her to be a class or two beneath him. On Valentine's Day, someone – it was rumoured that it was her father, who intensely disliked Albert – sent her a Valentine card with a verse written by hand: *Philomena dear you are so cute, but with this fact I won't dispute. Albert is a little villain. He's courting you, likewise the million.*

Whether the relationship would have foundered anyway is difficult to say, but certainly Philomena, being the sensible girl she was, took the message to heart and the relationship ended as quickly as it had begun.

Days passed, weeks passed, months passed with little or no headway having been made regarding unearthing rightful heirs. Ever so gradually, almost imperceptibly, the residents of Caplin Scull gave up their dream of receiving "manna from heaven" and for comfort fell back on the old adage, "If it sounds too good to be true, it probably is."

Actually, it was information that had filtered in from relatives in Boston which had finally doused their dreams and great expectations. Those relatives related horror stories in their letters about the heir-hunters' racket and how such people – swindlers, they said; mostly lawyers – bilked money out of innocent and unsuspecting people. They explained that while many such searches are legitimate, most are not.

This information was timely. By now many prospective heirs in the village had been contacted and asked to contribute a small sum of money – twenty-five dollars – per household to help defray the cost of the search. What the heir-hunters did not know was that they might as well have asked for twenty-five million for all the possibility they had of getting twenty-five dollars from anyone in Caplin Scull. Twenty-five dollars was a magnificent sum and not within the reach of most households. Also, hot on the heels of the request for donations, a rumour made the rounds that the period of dormancy had run its course and the money had reverted to the State of Massachusetts.

As well, World War II had just gotten underway and most of the young men in Caplin Scull were joining one branch or another of the military forces, or the auxiliary services, such as the Merchant Marines and Forestry Services. There was also talk the United States was going to join forces with the British and the Canadians and that Newfoundland was one of the places selected to set up offshore bases. This would mean work for all and sundry.

Soon the talk at wakes and weddings turned from the million to more urgent topics – who had signed up, who had been wounded and who had been killed, and the probability of bases being built on the island.

The subject of the million could no longer be likened to a fire on the dry blueberry barrens. It sputtered out, ember by ember as if it were being nurtured by wet spruce. On the rare occasions when the topic did come up, someone would invariably say reproachfully, "What fools we were. Everyone knows that the lot of the Newfoundlander is to work hard, die hard, and go to hell afterward. No free money is going to come our way unless we earn it by the sweat of our brow."

## The Farewell

A dozen or so houses make up the village. All flat-topped. All clapboarded. Their backs press up against the jagged cliff in order to make room for the rutted gravel road that snakes along the route of the land-wash and which dodges boulders and outcrops of razor-sharp rocks along the way. The road peters out at Martha's house. It peters out here because at this point the cliff is too steep and too bald to be of use to anyone. Had it continued on, however, it would have nudged up against Martha's front door.

Her house is perched on stilts in order to allow the Atlantic Ocean to flow underneath it whenever the tide is high enough to seep in through the leaky beach. This is an occurrence that can happen at any time but particularly in the spring. Martha's sheep house is also perched on stilts and during March and April there are many days when the sheep have to stay indoors and Martha has to wade through frothy sea water to feed them.

On this day, June 12, 1934, the land is dry and the tide is low. The sheep, seven in all, move clumsily about on the beach, nibbling tufts of grass that grow pale and salty around the rocks. From time to time they wander back to Martha's house to stare expectantly at its ochre-painted porch door. They wait for Martha to bring them their treat of bran meal, which she holds sack-like in her blue-checked apron. She does this every morning and she always stays around long enough to make sure the timid ones get their fair share.

But on this morning she does not come to the sheep house. She has more important things to do inside. She is in her kitchen, bent over her cast-iron stove, bullying a large chunk of green spruce to get it to settle down into the blazing kindling. With a sooty poker, she makes several fierce jabs at the piece of wet wood. When it finally catches on fire, she straightens up and hollers in the direction of the wash porch.

"Ye'd better get a move on, b'y, if yer goin' to catch that train. 'Tis nearin' eight already."

"I'll be in directly," Kevin shouts back. "I'm almost done."

Martha turns her attention to the fatback pork she is rendering out in the uneven-bottomed frying pan. As she carefully turns over each strip of pork to ensure that it is done crisp and golden – just the way Kevin likes it – she wishes she had something special to cook for him this morning, his last one with her. She would like for him to have something to boast about when he meets up with former Newfoundlanders now living in Boston, fishermen all. In her mind's ear she can hear him say, "B'ys oh b'ys, ye should have seen the feed Ma cooked fer me the mornin' I left to come here. Ye'd swear she thought there was a famine underway in the United States."

She sighs resignedly and comforts herself by spending extra time on preparing his usual breakfast: three slices of homemade bread, toasted on the back burners of the stove, and two eggs fresh from the henhouse. These she fries hard in the fat from the rendered-out salt pork.

She crosses the kitchen several times, walking between the stove and the breakfast table that is beside the front-facing window. Each trip back to the stove she flips the eggs from one side to the other and makes certain the toast is toasting, not simply scorching, and each trip back to the table, she adds to the dishes already on it – a plate she has heated in the oven until it is so hot she has to wrap her hand in the tail of her apron before taking hold of it, a salt shaker from the shelf behind the stove, kept there away from the dampness, a jug of molasses she had earlier brought out from the unheated pantry and had laid on top of the oven to thin it to pouring consistency.

Her steps are slower than usual this morning. She is stiff and sore from having sat up most of the night in the hard-backed rocker patching last-minute things to tuck into Kevin's suitcase. She surmises he will never wear half the stuff she has piled in there. But it does not matter. Just knowing he will have plenty of homespun socks and several changes of salt-water-thickened mitts to keep him warm is enough to make up for her complaining limbs.

She will never see him again once he leaves. She is certain of this. Such has been the case with her other four children who went to the United States. It was the case with Jack, who had left home at eighteen. With Gordon, who had just turned twenty. With the twins, Helen and Marie, who had only been eighteen – too young to be out on their own. They were too young to be servant girls in Boston but too old to expect their widowed mother to support them. It had been likewise with the children of other widowed mothers in the village.

Once they left they never returned. Not that anyone could blame them for never returning. Martha is quick to point this out, even to herself. How could they afford to return? As often as not they had borrowed their passage money from someone in the village and paying it back took every spare cent. And even though they were working in Boston, fishermen's wages there were still only fishermen's wages. And housemaids were still only housemaids. And with the Depression in full swing, money was almost as scarce in the United States as it was in Newfoundland.

But even knowing all of this, and as much as she wants her youngest child to stay home with her, she realizes it is in his own best interest to leave. At least in Boston he will be able to get work on the fishing boats. If he were to stay in Newfoundland and be unable to bring in any wages, he would soon lose pride in himself. Like many before him in the same situation, he might turn to the hop beer to deaden his soul. She has seen it happen many times.

\* \* \* \* \*

Kevin lingers in the porch. He lingers so long the water in the enamel pan is cold and he is tired of looking at his reflection in the cracked mirror. But he dreads going into the kitchen. What will they say to each other over breakfast? Every other morning their conversations have been the same – humdrum things that can be said when each person knows there is plenty of time to waste on trifling conversation: Is the sun going to break through the fog before the day is over so the new-mown hay can be turned or winnowed? Is there enough heat in the air so yesterday's freshly washed wool can be spread out on the rocks to dry? Is he going to be able to put out in the dory or will he have to wait until the wind settles down? She would always add that she did not want him to be like "No-Sense" Charlie who pulled out from shore no matter that his dory bobbed around in the waves like a cork from a bottle of rum. They always talked about the animals. He would ask if she had fed the sheep, knowing full well that she had. She would ask about Maisy, the cow, wondering if this was going to be one of her contrary days and she would not stand still for the milking.

This morning, however, these bits and pieces of conversation no longer seem relevant. The cow and the dory have been sold. The meadows have been leased to No-Sense Charlie and the sheep would be gone before the day was over.

Kevin pulls his father's watch from the side pocket of his grey flannel pants. He cannot put off going into the kitchen any longer. He peers one last time into the yellowed, spider-tracked mirror over the washstand and then straightens his collar even though it doesn't need straightening.

Martha hears him opening the porch door but she does not look up. She places the plate of eggs at his end of the table and then walks back to the stove. They pass each other in the centre of the kitchen floor. After she needlessly pokes the wood in the brightly burning fire, she takes the teapot from a back burner of the stove and brings it to the table and pours his tea. She pours a cup for herself and sits opposite him.

He fumbles around for something to say. He catches sight of her heavy black shawl and her head scarf bunched up on a stool. He sees her outdoor boots, along with his, warming underneath the stove.

He points to the huddle of clothes. "What've you got that out fer?" His voice is tight, angry even.

She takes a sip of tea and lays the cup carefully down in its saucer. "I'm walkin' as far as the station with ye." Her voice is as tight as his.

"'Deed yer not," he snaps. "There's no need to go out in this cold fog. That's a bunch of foolishness. Next thing ye knows ye'll be laid up sick. I might even have to come back home to look after ye."

She retorts in the same starchy voice. "A bunch of foolishness or not, I'm goin' jest the same. That's if ye ever gets around to eatin' yer breakfast. Ye moved faster when ye were goin' to yer father's funeral."

He begins to eat, carefully chopping his eggs into squares with his fork, concentrating hard as if it were important to get each square to be of equal size.

She sips her tea, cupping the cup with both hands. She stares out through the window. She says the water is terribly choppy, but wouldn't you know it, No-Sense Charlie is out there in his little punt of a dory.

He says she better not forget about the fellow from the Jersey Side who is coming in the afternoon to buy the sheep. She replies that if she couldn't remember that much she had better put her name in for a bed in the lunatic asylum in St. John's.

He reaches toward the windowsill for the can of Prince Albert tobacco that he always keeps there. He rolls a cigarette and then starts to put the can back on the sill. After a slight hesitation he stuffs it into his back trouser pocket. He glances at the clock.

"I'll smoke this at the station," he says, nodding towards the cigarette, as he hurriedly gets up from the table as if he has just realized that time has gotten away from him.

She, too, glances at the clock. "'Tis high time all right. Best we were on our way."

He goes to the porch to get his overcoat.

She picks up her boots and begins to slowly pull them on. It is as if each one weighs a ton.

\* \* \* \* \*

The road leading from the house is rocky and in places it is still humped up from the frost heaves in May. Martha picks her way carefully. For once Kevin does not show impatience at her slowness. He even attempts to match his gait to hers.

She says, her voice challenging, "I finished a pair of socks fer ye last night. A waste of time, I s'pose. Ye'll be too proud to wear homespuns in Boston."

"No I won't," he replies, his tone as short as hers. "Not if it gets cold enough."

He hurriedly pats his suit coat pocket. "I left me razor behind. I meant to carry it in me pocket so I'd have it handy for the train." He rummages in his pants pockets. "I left it fer sure."

"That you did," she says. "On the washstand. Try lookin' in yer overcoat pocket."

His brown twill overcoat, a second-hand one his brother had sent home to him for the trip, is slung over his left arm. He sets his new cardboard suitcase down on the ground while he searches in his overcoat pockets. Finding the bulge of the razor, he confirms, "'Tis there all right."

"Because I put it there," she snaps. "Ye'd ferget yer head if it weren't connected to yer neck."

He fumbles with his suitcase, picking it up and brushing the mud off the bottom. He wishes he was already on the train. He wishes the train was already pulling out of the station.

She wishes likewise.

"No need to come any further," he says gruffly. "The road's goin' to be even worse further along. Might break an ankle if ye don't watch it."

"Yes, 'tis far enough," she agrees, but makes no attempt to turn back.

"Don't ferget the fellow comin' fer the sheep," he reminds her, inching ahead of her. "And get Tom's boy to help with the firewood."

"Don't you ferget to write. And don't go puttin' on airs when ye comes home next summer," knowing many summers will have passed by the time he returns.

"Not likely," he says with exaggerated annoyance. "Don't expect to have much to put on airs about."

She shivers and hauls her shawl tighter around her stooped shoulders.

"See!" he admonishes. "Yer already catching yer death."

"So I am, b'y. I'd better get back."

She looks at him, but makes certain not to meet his eyes. "Well, farewell to ye, b'y. Snow to yer heels and wind at yer back."

"Yeah, okay. Farewell to ye, too."

He gives a quick offhand wave and the tail of his overcoat dips into the mud.

"Pick up yer overcoat," she orders. "It won't be fit to wear by the time ye gets to Boston."

He hitches the overcoat higher on his shoulder and gives another quick wave.

"Farewell to ye, Ma."

"Farewell to ye, b'y."

\* \* \* \* \*

Martha trudges back to her house. She walks slowly. There is no need to hurry. She picks up an old spruce stick along the path and uses it for a walking cane, leaning heavily on it so that it sinks deep into the soft spring ground. She laments out loud as she walks.

"Everything's gone now. Everything but the sheep. And they'll be gone by evening."

She recalls the day she had received the news that her husband had been drowned off the Grand Banks. "Him only forty-four. And me with a houseful of small children." She remembers when young Willie had died of pneumonia. She was sure at the time that she had been given more grief than she could bear, but she had to keep going for the sake of the remaining children.

When she gets near her house she hears the sheep bleating. "Ye poor beasts," she exclaims, her hand rushing to her mouth. "I've forgotten all about ye. I haven't given ye a bite to eat yet. Not one morsel."

She goes directly to the sheep house. As she takes a bundle of hay from the rack and places it in the feeder, the train whistle blows. The sound of it lances through her body, bringing with it such pain she has to lean against the hayrack to keep from falling. For several minutes she remains leaning up against the rack, her forehead pressed hard into the rough boards to keep herself from crying.

It suddenly dawns on her that there is no longer any reason to keep up a front. She can finally cry. She can cry for the ones who are dead and for the ones who are in the United States and who are as lost to her as if they were already dead.

The train chugs its way out of the village. The sound of it gets fainter and fainter as it rounds bend after bend. When she can hear it no more, she straightens up, dry-eyed.

"What's the good of crying?" she asks, as if the sheep will supply her with an answer. "'Tis jest a waste of me strength."

The sheep have clustered around her trying to nibble at the hay in the feeder. She looks at them all, each one special. Each one loved. She looks at the one she has reared from a lamb when its mother died giving birth. She looks at the one she calls Patch because of the black spot on his face.

She pushes them gently aside with her leg.

"Move away, ye ugly brutes, so I can get out of here. Tomorrow ye'll be someone else's problem."

She pulls her shawl closer around her shoulders and heads back to her empty house.

## *Viewing Not Advised*

They had to take out the parlour window and pry off a couple of clapboards to get Harry O'Reilly's casket inside his mother's house. And they had to hack off most of the branches of the lilac tree which grew just outside the parlour window. Everyone said that cutting back the tree was a real shame because only yesterday it had come into full purple bloom. But there was no other way; the branches were so ungainly they completely blocked the entrance to the window.

Mrs. Josie, Harry's mother, wanted her son brought in through her front door as would be befitting any slain soldier. However, she had failed to take into account the professionally made casket that had been freighted out from the military hospital in St. John's. It was so much larger than anything that would have been cobbled together in Caplin Scull that it was impossible to squeeze it in through the narrow front door. Besides, after it cleared the front door, it still had to be hoisted over the staircase banister in order to line it up with the parlour door – a precarious job, even for a half-dozen men. There was no way around it. The casket had to come in through the parlour window.

Within an hour of his early evening arrival, Harry was set up in the parlour, his casket resting on four straight-backed kitchen chairs. Two candles – special ones blessed by the priest on Candlemas Day – had been lit and placed on a small table at the head of the casket. A pickle bottle, overflowing with the lilac blooms that had been salvaged from the hacked-off branches, was on another small table at the foot of the casket.

Mrs. Josie fussed around the casket, tenderly draping the Union Jack over it and gently tugging on it to make certain it fell in even folds to the floor. She then took Harry's watch from her apron pocket, rubbed her hand over it as if in a caress, and placed it on top of the Union Jack.

The watch had belonged to her husband. Harry had only been a little boy when his father died in the lumber woods and he had claimed that watch for his own. He never left it out of his sight. He even took it to the war with him and someone who had visited him in the military hospital in St. John's said he had it laid on his bedside table, within a hand's reach of his bed.

When the makeshift viewing room was in readiness – the candles lit, the casket draped, the mats fluffed – Mrs. Josie laid her rosary beads beside the watch, on the exact spot where Harry's hands were surmised to be folded, and Father Mullaly, the parish priest, led the gathering in the praying of the rosary for the repose of Harry's soul. He then took his leave, saying he had to get back to the rectory in time for Friday evening devotions.

When night fell, Mrs. Josie went up to her bedroom, exhausted from the day, leaving the wake keepers with the kitchen all to themselves. As soon as they heard the creaking of her bed springs, assuring them she would not be back downstairs again until morning, they set about livening up the place.

Mary Frances, a neighbour, and Bridget Cleary, Harry's young girlfriend, began preparing vegetables for the pot of salt beef that was already in full boil on the stove. Earlier in the day, Phonse, the oldest of the wake keepers, had smuggled in a keg of home-brew and had hidden it under the kitchen table. He now pulled it out into the centre of the kitchen and invited the other pallbearers – Mrs. Josie's brother-in-law, Austin Lannon; Harry's best friend, Neddie Nolan; and Mary Frances's brother, Gussie Tobin – to fill up their glasses.

"C'mon, b'ys," Phonse said, releasing the bung from the keg. "Let's get a few drinks into ourselves so things'll look brighter."

He singled out Neddie. "Me son, yer not here jest fer yer good looks. Pick up that accordion and give us a tune."

"Yes, b'y," Austin seconded. "We needs things livened up a bit. In honour of Harry, play the Regiment's tune."

Neddie began playing "The Banks of Newfoundland" and Phonse, holding aloft his full glass of beer, got up and step-danced around the beer keg while the beer from his held-aloft glass sloshed to the floor. At the end of the tune, he dropped back into his chair, exhausted, and Neddie laid his accordion aside.

"Don't put that thing away, Neddie!" Mary Frances ordered. "Bridget is goin' to give us a song. Ent ye, Bridget?"

Bridget shook her head. "I don't feel much like singin'. Not right now."

"Sure you do, girl," Austin coaxed. "Sing Harry's song. Sing 'Come Back, Paddy 'Reilly.'"

"Come on, me love," Phonse cajoled. "We all loves that song."

Mary Frances laid aside the turnip she was peeling and clapped encouragement. "C'mon, me darlin', sing 'Come Back, Paddy 'Reilly.'"

She began to coax off-tune and just above a whisper. "The Garden of Eden has vanished they say ..."

Neddie played a few bars of the tune, warming up. Reluctantly, Bridget began to sing, her voice unsteady. Austin and Phonse swayed their beer glasses, keeping time to the music.

> The Garden of Eden has vanished they say
> But I know the lie of it still
> Just turn to the left at the Bridge of Finea
> And stop when halfway to Cootehill.
> 'Tis there I will find it I know sure enough
> When fortune has come to my call
> O the grass it is green around Ballyjamesduff
> And the blue sky is over it all.

Bridget's voice quavered and Phonse hurriedly waved everyone to join in.

"C'mon, fellows. Join in. Help her out."

They all obliged and chimed in on the chorus.

*And tones that are tender and tones that are gruff*
*Come whispering over the sea*
*Come back, Paddy 'Reilly, to Ballyjamesduff*
*Come home Paddy 'Reilly, to me.*

Bridget began to sob uncontrollably and Mary Frances went to comfort her. She put an arm around her shoulders.

"There, there, me darlin'. Let it all come out. You've a right to that. Not bein' able to see him even in death. That's the hard part. And you two were as close as peas in a pod. As young as ye were it was plain ye were meant fer each other."

Austin pushed himself up out of his chair and went to refill his beer glass. *"Viewing Not Advised,"* he said scornfully. "That's a bunch of bloody horseshit. Who in the hell do they think they are tellin' us we can't see our own Harry! We should be able to lift that lid if it bloody well pleases us."

Phonse quickly backed him up. "I'm with you there, b'y. We should be able to see him. He went away August 1914 and here it is June 1919. Never clapped eyes on him in between."

"Think … think … think twice about openin' him up, b'ys," Gussie Tobin advised, stuttering his words in the way he had of doing whenever he was excited or frightened. "'Tis bad luck to open up a casket."

"Bad luck or good luck. All the same difference to me," Mary Frances pronounced. "Not while I have an ounce of strength in me body will ye open him up."

She swept her gaze over the four men in the manner she had of making her statements final. She then went to the stove and lifted the cover on the salt beef pot. With a long two-pronged fork, she jabbed at the hunk of meat to determine how near it was to being cooked.

"Falling apart, almost," she said with satisfaction. "Time to get the turnips in."

She addressed Bridget. "Too bad, girl, you and Mrs. Josie couldn't have gotten in to see him this spring after he was sent back from that hospital in England. But I knows well enough about the expense. Ye'd have to stay a week in St. John's on account of the train. Everythin' costs money."

Bridget wiped her eyes with the back of her hand. "Sure they kept tellin' us Harry was doin' as well as could be expected." Her voice was as bitter as gall. "That's what the letters they wrote for him said. The nurses wrote them. If we'd known he was at death's door, we'd have found the money from somewhere to go see him."

"Sure you would," Phonse consoled. "They kept the truth from you." He mimicked the information the nurses in the military hospital had written to Mrs. Josie. "'Yer son is doin' as well as can be expected.'"

"Ye'd get more information out of a horse's asshole," he said derisively. "'As well as can be expected.' Expected for what? For a dyin' man? For a corpse?"

He waved his empty glass at Austin, who was lumbering across the floor, heading for the keg of beer.

"While yer up, b'y, fill mine up, too. And I say let's open up Harry as soon as we gets a few more beers into us. Hell's flames with the government and 'Viewing Not Advised.'"

He nodded his head in Mary Frances's direction to include her with those faceless others who had determined that Harry should not be viewed. "Hell's flames with the lot of them."

Mary Frances was stooped over a counter chopping up a head of cabbage. She quickly straightened up and jabbed her cutting knife in the air in Austin's direction.

"Not while I have a breath in me body will ye open him up!"

She looked towards the ceiling, beyond which was Mrs. Josie's bedroom.

"Ye ent goin' to hurt that poor soul any more than she's already been hurt. Her youngest child dead and she blames herself. She says if she hadn't signed Harry's enlistment papers, he couldn't have gone to the war, him bein' underage. But he pestered her so much she finally gave in.

"Get some sense into you, woman," Austin said testily. "How can it hurt her to see her own son? Besides, we don't have to let her in on what we're doin'. We'll jest nail him back up after we gets a look."

"You're the one who needs to get sense," Mary Frances retorted. "Maybe he's all smashed up. Ever think of that? The hospital wouldn't have put that sign on the casket 'Viewing Not Advised' if there hadn't been a good reason."

Again she pointed to the ceiling. "No need to place more guilt on that poor soul's heart than is already there."

Phonse quickly interjected. "I tried to get her to stop blamin' herself. I said if she wants to blame anyone, blame the Newfoundland government – sendin' our young boys overseas to spill their blood on foreign soil." He added scornfully, "And for *England*! I bet no one in England could find Caplin Scull on a map if you gave them a magnifyin' glass. And I bet they don't know Harry 'Reilly is lyin' dead in that parlour in the prime of his life. All on their account. England wouldn't spare a cup of piss for all of Newfoundland even if our lives depended on it."

Neddie seconded Phonse's pronouncement. "And hundreds more than Harry got slaughtered. Bill Ryan's father told me that at the Battle of the Somme – and that's where Harry met his comeuppance and where his brother, Jack, got killed – the bullets were as thick as hailstones. He said Bill told him he turned up his collar and marched forward as if the turned-up collar could protect him, as if he were home in Caplin Scull and was walkin' head-on into a sleet storm."

Austin reached for Neddie's glass. "Might as well fill up yers, Neddie, while I'm up here."

He sniffed the air appreciatively and looked in the direction of the pot of salt beef and vegetables.

"Beginnin' to smell some good, Mary Frances." He held up Neddie's full glass of beer for inspection. "And this beer tastes some good, too."

"Yes, good beer all right," Neddie allowed, "but don't swell Phonse's head with too much praise. Meself, I feels so good right now, I'm convinced we should open up Harry right this blessed minute and let him get a sniff of homebrew and a whiff of that salt beef and cabbage."

He turned to Bridget, hoping to bring her onside. "You'd like to see him, too, wouldn't you, girl?"

"Sure I would," she said, her voice heavy with sorrow. "Ye knows very well I would, but the government said the casket was sealed and we shouldn't tamper with it. And ye saw the notice on the casket that the hospital put on. And the telegram from the government said the same thing, 'Viewing Not Advised.' Why would they put that on the casket unless he was all smashed up or somethin'? Or had a disease."

"The *government*," Neddie mocked, slapping his hands against his twisted knees, twisted from a birth deformity. "We should give a pinch of hen shit about the government? Did it care about Mrs. Josie when they took Harry away to be slaughtered? And I'd be slaughtered, too, if it hadn't been for these crooked legs here. I knows very well I'd have gone with Harry. Me and him were good buddies. That's why I'd like so much to see him."

"Here's to Neddie's crooked legs," Phonse said, hoisting aloft his glass of beer. "It kept him from bein' shot to hell in France. And I'm with him when he says let's open up Harry so he can have one last look around."

He looked towards Mary Frances. "Don't ye think he'd want to take one last look at the pictures on the wall? His father. His brother Jack in uniform. Himself, fer that matter, in uniform."

Mary Frances faced down the four men. "Now listen here, ye fellows. Jest because yer bellies are filled with hop beer is no reason fer ye to do somethin' foolish. Yer not openin' that casket and that's it! Ye saw the sign on it. 'Sealed,' it said. And like Bridget said, ye read the telegram. It said, 'Viewing Not Advised.' That was said for some reason."

"Who pays attention to that stuff, girl?" Austin Lannon sneered. "I bet the government says that to everyone. Jim Barnes' boy had the same thing on his box. Meself, I thinks the government probably had to get somethin' for some of their lackies to do, so they had them make up a whole bunch of stickers sayin' 'Viewing Not Advised' and some others sayin' 'Sealed' and then they had to use them somewhere. Ye knows how it goes with the government. Got to hide the waste. There are more people with nothin' to do but sit on their arses on government chairs than there are lice on a gannet."

At that moment, a flash of lightning shot in through the kitchen window, followed by a loud clap of thunder. Mary Frances made a rapid sign of the cross over herself.

"Blessed Lord. There 'tis. The storm they threatened. And all the windows in the house are wide open. Every last one."

She started for the hall door that led to the upstairs bedrooms. She stopped and beckoned to Bridget.

"Give me a hand, girl. If the casings get wet, they'll swell twice their size and we'll never get the bloody things closed."

Bridget quickly got up and followed Mary Frances up the stairs.

As soon as the door closed behind the two women, Phonse jumped to his feet.

"Now's our time, b'ys. I knows where Mrs. Josie keeps her crowbars and stuff. Just out here in the back shed."

He raced out through the kitchen door, followed by Austin. Within a couple of seconds they returned, each one carrying a crowbar. Austin also had a hammer and a chisel. He handed the hammer to Neddie and the chisel to Gussie, who lamely protested having to take part in what was about to happen. He was squeamish when it came to dead bodies. And he was a believer in ghosts and the supernatural and the right of the dead not to be disturbed. Still, he took the chisel and followed the others into the parlour.

"This'll do it, b'ys." Austin said, brandishing the crowbar as he headed for the parlour. "Hurry! We haven't much time."

Within a few minutes, the casket was pried open. Gussie quickly turned his head aside and moved away. Austin, Phonse, and Neddie peeked inside it.

"Sweet Redeemer! Sweet Saviour! Oh, Mother of God!" Phonse said, his voice strangled. He staggered away from the casket and dropped into a chair. Neddie and Austin remained looking in at the body as if they were riveted to the spot.

When Mary Frances came back downstairs she had to pass the open parlour door. She heard the commotion in the room. She saw the raised lid on the casket. She saw Phonse slumped in a chair. She saw Neddie and Austin staring at the corpse, staring as if they were transfixed.

"Oh, Merciful Mother! Oh, Hand of God! Ye drunken fools!" she hissed. "Ye went and opened it."

Scowling, she strode across the room, towards the casket, past Phonse, who was still sitting as if stupefied in his chair.

"Ent him!" Phonse mumbled as she passed by. He spoke without looking at her.

"Don't talk so foolish, b'y." Mary Frances dismissed him and kept on going into the room. She stopped beside the casket and looked in. She saw the body of a young man dressed in the uniform of the Newfoundland Regiment.

She grabbed her heart. "Oh, Holy Saint Joseph! Oh, Immaculate Heart of Mary! Oh, Sacred Heart Divine!" She then made a rapid sign of the cross over herself as she reeled back against the wall. "Oh, Joseph Most Chaste! Ent him. Fer sure, it ent him."

Having followed Mary Frances down the stairs, Bridget halted in the parlour doorway. Phonse, seeing her, roused himself from his stupor and reached out both arms to try to stop her from coming any further.

"Go back, girl! Don't look at him. Fer the love of Christ, don't look at him. Ent Harry a-tall. Nothin' like him."

Bridget paid no attention. She hurried to the casket.

Mary Frances tried to waylay her. "Don't! Don't! Don't!" she said fiercely, wringing her hands as if the gates of hell had opened up before her and she had to decide whether to step through or not. "A total stranger in there."

Bridget rushed toward the casket and looked in. She gulped air in short, hitching mouthfuls. Her hands rushed to her face. She started to sway backwards. "Ohohoh! Ohohoh!"

Neddie grabbed her and eased her down into a chair. Mary Frances went to her side. "Water, b'ys. Water," she said in spurts, gasping for air as if she were a fish stranded on land. "Get us some water. Gentle Saviour! Can't blame her a bit for faintin'. 'Tis enough to give anyone a bit of a turn."

"I'm takin' that booze pledge as soon as I gets out of here," Gussie Tobin mumbled. He was standing at the far end of the parlour, as far as he could get away from the casket without leaving the room. "I'm even willin' to own up to Mullaly that I'm a drunk." He kept his hands over his eyes in case he happened to glance in the vicinity of the casket. "Cold sober I'd never have been part of this."

Phonse was the first to get himself under control. "Close him up, b'ys. And hold our tongues." He said this as he got up and moved toward the casket, stooping down to pick up the hammer that was lying on the floor alongside the crowbar and chisel. "If Mrs. Josie finds out, the shock might kill her."

Neddie nodded his assent. He alone had remained standing beside the casket, unable to take his gaze from the corpse. "Better fer everyone if we sez nothin'." He grasped the casket lid to pull it closed. "Not a word to anyone. Do ye hear?" he said, his eyes taking in all five of them. "Not a word! Close him up and pretend he's Harry. Pull the Union Jack over the whole bloody thing."

"No!" Bridget shouted, struggling to get out of her chair to block the closing of the casket with her body. "We have to find Harry. We have to let them know that Buddy in there ent Harry."

"She's right, b'ys," Mary Frances agreed. She, too, moved towards the casket and once more looked down upon the corpse. "He ent Harry. No way we can convince ourselves he is. But like she says, we have to own up. We can't let Mrs. Josie bury a complete stranger thinking he's her son."

"But if we tells her about the mix-up, it might kill her," Phonse objected. "Besides, like Neddie said, he's got to go in the ground tomorrow." He held his nostrils between his finger and thumb. "He's already beginnin' to go."

"Should've thought of that before ye sprung it open."

Mary Frances' tone held no sympathy for their predicament, which at this moment she did not realize was also her predicament. "Pack Buddy right back to St. John's is what I say. Exchange him for Harry."

"That's the right thing to do," Bridget said eagerly. "If we sit here and pretend he's our Harry, no one will go lookin'."

She got up and walked towards the casket. As she did so, she added a serious obstacle to passing the stranger off as Harry if any of them had a notion to do that.

"Have ye fellows considered that Buddy here might be a Protestant? We can't bury a Protestant in a Catholic cemetery. We could be excommunicated for that. Ye jest got to own up to what ye did and send him back."

"Send – Buddy – back!" Phonse repeated slowly, looking at Bridget as if she had lost her mind. "Where's yer head, girl? How can we send him back? The train don't come for six more days. If we keeps him here in the parlour that long – from Friday to Friday – there won't be enough Jeyes Fluid in Murphy's store to cut the stench."

"He's right," Austin said. "And it's not like we had a car and could strap him on the roof. No one in Caplin Scull has a car."

"They're right, girl," Neddie quickly agreed, staring down at Buddy. He pointed at the corpse. "He's leakin' at the mouth." He pulled his thumb and index finger down the sides of his own mouth as if wiping away putrefaction.

Austin, too, stared down at the body, sombrely scrutinizing it. He latched onto a solution.

"Have ye given it any thought that perhaps 'tis Harry and we don't recognize him? Ye knows how war changes people. And he's several years older than when we last saw him."

"Don't be so foolish, Austin," Mary Frances snapped. "Of course he ent Harry. That poor divil in there has a nose on him as long as the Burin Peninsula. Longer than the month of March."

She pointed to Harry's photograph that was hanging on the wall above the casket, the one Harry had taken in St. John's just before he had gotten his orders to leave for England.

"Besides, Harry was as freckly faced as a tom cod. And he had red hair, like his father before him, Lord have mercy on his soul." She quickly turned her gaze back to the casket, and asked cantankerously, "Do any of ye see freckles or any sign of red hair on Buddy here?"

Each one shook his head. Phonse closed the casket lid slowly but made no attempt to hammer it shut. Each one of them slumped down into the parlour chairs.

"In the name of Jesus, what are we goin' to do," Austin said. It was a statement, not a question. "We're in some kind of mess now. Some kind of bloody mess."

"A bloody mess fer sure," Phonse agreed. "And I jest thought of something else. If we tells Mullaly that Buddy ent Harry, he won't allow him to be buried in the cemetery, even if we offer to dig a new grave. We don't know whether that fellow is even a Christian, much less a Catholic, so he'll have to be put outside the cemetery fence. Like a bloated horse. And no soldier deserves that treatment."

Neddie agitatedly slapped his hands along one side of his crooked legs. "I'd rather be in jail than be in the fix we're in now. But like ye sez, even if we owns up, we still can't keep Buddy in the parlour for a week waitin' for the train to come. We can't even wait for the weekend to be over." He curled his lip.

"Ye fellows ever smell meat that's gone off? I worked one summer in a slaughterhouse in Avondale. Kills the appetite, that's fer sure."

Bridget, certain that she had found a way out, said, hopefully, "We could send a telegram to the military hospital. Then they could start lookin' fer Harry right away. Fer sure ye'll have to own up to what ye did fer that to happen. But ye did no worse than the government did when they sent out the wrong body."

"Telegraph offices are closed on Saturdays," Austin reminded her, sharply. "Ye knows that as well as I do. Tomorrow is Saturday. Today is Friday."

Sensing that the situation was getting more hopeless with every suggested solution, Austin tried to calm things down.

"Besides, girl, what can the hospital do? They can't make the train come any faster. And how in the hell are they goin' to find Harry? He's most likely buried by now under some other name. Unless he's in an ice house somewhere. Or wherever they keep bodies that have to hang over. What do you expect us to do? Go to that ice house and pry open fifteen or twenty caskets, hoping one of them is Harry? And it might be all fer nothin'. That fellow jest might be Harry and he looks different dead. And in uniform."

"Fer all we knows," Mary Frances said, "Buddy in there might be from up the Coasts. Harry in his stead might be on a mail boat right this minute on his way to St. Anthony's. It's goin' to take a long time to get this mess untangled. And in the meantime, what about poor Mrs. Josie? She got a grave that's waitin' to be filled."

She then gave a scathing look at each man. "Ye

liquored-up fools, ye got us into some bloody mess. If ye had left the box closed, Buddy in there would be Harry."

"Yer right, girl," Neddie agreed. "And it mightn't be a one-fer-one swap. Like one 'Reilly mistaken fer another 'Reilly. What if he's a different person altogether? We can't very well go around to every boneyard in Newfoundland lookin' fer new graves and sayin' when we finds one, 'Up she comes, b'ys. That might be our Harry down there. Then agin it might not. It might be yer son.'"

He swiped his hand across his forehead and down his perspiration-coated cheeks. Within a minute he jumped up as if he had just been given the definitive answer. He hobbled across the floor and grabbed the hammer that was lying beside the casket.

"I'm goin' to hammer him shut. As far as everyone is concerned, we never opened him up. 'Tis the only way out."

"Yes, hammer him shut," Mary Frances said. "We can't have Mrs. Josie spendin' days and weeks and months lookin' into that yawnin' grave waitin' fer Harry to show up."

Bridget let out a loud wail. "Ye can't do that. We got to send him back so we can find Harry. Harry mightn't even be dead."

Austin shook his head, negating any credibility in what she was saying.

"He's dead, girl. Put that notion out of yer head. Even the government wouldn't make that much of a mistake. They wouldn't say an alive man was dead if he wasn't. Meself, I thinks the coffins jest got switched when they were puttin' the addresses on.

But who was Harry switched with? That's an answer we're not likely to get. Could be John Smith. Or Jack Callagan. Or Louis Levinski. Lots of Levinskis in St. John's. Buddy could be a Levinski." He gave a mischievous chuckle. "Peter Fitzgerald is next door to Harry's grave. He hated all of the Levinskis because they were more successful merchants than he was."

Gussie Tobin, who felt unsettled just by having the open casket in the parlour, tried for a quick remedy to the situation.

"Like Mary Frances said, he could be Harry even if he don't look like him. Harry was rail thin and this fellow has a pair of shoulders on him like Murphy's scow. But for all we know, Harry may have grown a pair of shoulders."

Bridget spoke up. "I've been thinkin'," she said. "That fellow just might be Harry. There was his father's watch that was sent out with his body. How could someone else get his watch? I'm beginnin' to think he's Harry even if he looks nothin' like him."

"Good thinkin', girl," Gussie stammered. He picked up a hammer and moved quickly towards the casket. "Since, since, we all agrees he might be Harry even if he isn't Harry, we'll close him up and shut up about it. We'll bury him on Monday jest as if he were Harry." He held his hand over his heart. "Upon our souls, not a word to anyone. Certainly not to Mrs. Josie or to Mullaly. There's nothing else to be done."

Mary Frances held her hand over her heart. "I agree. Anythin' is better than havin' Mrs. Josie spend the rest of her days kneelin' beside that grave hole, waitin' fer Harry to own it. Besides, he has to be gotten out of this house by tomorrow. Now that he's been opened and the air has reached him, he'll go faster."

"Ya, good thinkin', girl," Phonse echoed Gussie.

Neddie shambled across the floor and grabbed up a hammer. "Yes. Hammer him shut. 'Tis the only way." He turned towards the casket. "As far as I'm concerned, that's Harry in there. I don't care if he looks more like a sculpin than Harry."

Bridget reluctantly relented. "If I can't find Harry without hurtin' Mrs. Josie, then I say go head and bury Buddy in Harry's grave. Rememberin' about that watch has changed me mind. We'll make believe 'tis Harry."

Unbeknownst to the others, Mrs. Josie had been standing in the doorway listening. "He's got to be given a proper burial," she said. "The hole is already dug. Say nothin' to no one. Whoever the poor devil is, he's some poor mother's son."

## The Return

I flew in the face of Thomas Wolfe's cautionary tale – the one that states you can't go home again – and I headed back to the surroundings of my childhood. I had been away from my tiny outport community on Newfoundland's southeast coast for so long I had no immediate kin left there. Even the tag ends of my family – first cousins and second cousins – had either moved away or died off.

I met Mildred just outside the one and only church in the area. Mildred had been an old woman when I was a child and now twenty years later she looked only slightly older. And only slightly more tattered.

"I remembers you," she said, in her thick Newfoundland Irish brogue when she came upon me as I walked along the road adjacent to the Roman Catholic church. In my absence this road had been elevated to the status of street, even though it was still just a narrow lane, haphazardly paved and hemmed in on either side by front yards and picket fences.

"Of course I remembers you," she assured me and to prove she did, she called me by name. "You were jest a young girl the last time I saw you. But I'd recognize you anywhere. From your mother's side of the family."

She was only faking remembering me, and she knew I knew that as well, so she decided to make a clean breast of things by immediately owning up to her lie.

"Girl, the truth is I probably wouldn't have recognized you if someone hadn't mentioned you were back."

She nodded her head in the direction of the Church of the Sacred Heart, large and ornate, which formed our backdrop and served not only the needs of this community but the needs of a cluster of surrounding villages as well, Caplin Scull being one.

"Jest came from there." She gestured toward the church. "From Confession. A strange priest here now."

In the idiom of the community, a strange priest meant a newcomer priest as opposed to the known priest and just to make conversation I asked how recently he had arrived.

"Jest came, girl. About a month ago. From the Congo. Or so they tells me that's where he's from." She gave a wry smile, displaying yellowed dentures with two missing plastic teeth. "Remember, girl, when we used to put money in the church envelopes every Sunday so our missionaries could go to the Congo to Christianize the pagans?"

I nodded that yes, I did remember. Only too well

I remembered my mother on Saturday night, searching pockets and purses for an unexpected quarter that she may have squirrelled away. The contribution envelope was divided into two pockets. One pocket was marked Foreign Missionaries, the other Church Upkeep. On Sundays when my mother would pass the envelope over to my father to take to church with him, he would look at the slack pocket and remark, "Lopsided again today, girl." Her answer never swerved. "The youngsters needed stuff fer school. The Vatican can look after the missionaries."

"Well, girl, everything changes," Millie informed me, bringing me back to the present. "The Congo people are now coming over here to Christianize us."

She gave a devilish smile. "I wonders if over there they're stuffin' envelopes with quarters to help us out over here. Bet they're not. Not that a quarter will go very far these days. Like I said, everyt'ing changes, girl. Sometimes fer the best. Sometimes not. 'Tis the way it 'tis."

Her face instantly soured, her lips pulled taut over the gapped teeth. "But I'll tell you one t'ing that won't change in a hurry and that's me promise to meself not to go to Confession to him again. Even if I burns in hell fer not goin'." She jerked her thumb in the direction of the church, the confessional, and the strange priest from the Congo.

"What happened?" I asked, anxious to hear what could have turned her off so badly. She wasn't the sort you would tag for having to confess sins salacious enough to be worthy of pastoral chastisement.

"Well," she said, "I goes into the Confession box and when he pulled the shutter back I says to him like I always says, 'Bless me, Fadder, fer I have sinned. I missed Mass on Sundays.'" She wrinkled her brow. "I thinks I even gave him a number. Yes, I'm sure I did. Four times, I said. 'I missed Mass four times, Fadder.' And without any further ado, like him askin' if I missed Mass without good reason, he says to me, 'Why are you wasting my time telling me this!' Girl, you could have knocked me over with a feather! Imagine! *Wasting his time confessing a mortal sin!* Who ever heard the *like*? So right then and there I sez to meself, 'My sonny b'y, the chamber pots'll be frozen solid before I'll darken yer door agin.'"

She waited for me to look shocked at all that she had related and my look of consternation must have accommodated her sufficiently because she continued.

"Imagine tellin' me I was wastin' his time when I had committed a mortal sin. In fact, four mortal sins! I missed Mass four times."

She held up four stubby fingers for emphasis. "I had no reason for missin' Mass. No *good* reason anyway. Neither of the times – April or June. It was cold and rainy, ye knows how these months are here, and of course I had to walk almost a mile to get here, and I'm headin' for eighty, so when I woke up on those Sunday mornin's and looked out at the weather, I jest said to meself, 'Shag it all, b'ys, no Mass fer me today. I'm stayin' home and huggin' the quilts."

She continued her verbal self-flagellation, exposing her great need to do penance for her dastardly deed. Even a Hail Mary or two would have sufficed.

"So that tells you I deliberately didn't go to Mass," she said. "On any of those Sundays. Don't it?

And it wasn't as if I don't know better. Because I do."

She gave me a baffled look. "Sure a strange way for a priest to act. Don't ye think? And not only that, girl, he's already done away with that beautiful white marble altar and put up a little wooden table instead. No more arses turned to the people. That's what he said. Or somet'ing along those lines. He didn't say arses of course. That's what they're doin' these days in Newfoundland. Facin' the congregation. I s'pose 'tis the same where you lives. That big council they held in Rome shook up everyt'ing. Don't know what himself did with that beautiful marble altar that he took out. Gone out of sight, that's all I knows. Probably smashed it to smithereens. Like Father Hines did with the statues and the stained-glass windows – smashed them to hell in the landwash." She held her thumb and forefinger apart, measuring off about a half-inch. "Not a piece bigger than that left."

She tapped the side of her head. "Only poor Father Hines was mental. Went right off the head he did. Thought the statues were keeping tabs on him when he was nippin' on the altar wine. It was a likin' fer the booze that did him in. He wasn't mental to start with. And I was sorry to see him leave. In some ways he did more fer us drunk than others had done sober. He shaped up our schools.

"But 'tis different with this fellow. He's sane enough. And as far as we knows, he's sober. But mark my words, girl, he's goin' to ransack the place before he leaves. Probably goin' to go back to the Congo with anyt'ing that's not hammered down or can fit in his suitcase."

She pursed her lips and lowered her voice to a

conspiratorial whisper. "Me darlin', jest between you and me, I thinks we wasted our money sendin' missionaries from here over to the Congo. Don't ye t'ink the ones they converted must've got the teachin' all backwards if they come over here sayin' there's nothin' wrong with committin' a mortal sin by missin' Mass? But in fairness, it might not have been intentional. I believes it might have somet'ing to do with them not fully understandin' the English language. That's the only t'ing I can put it down to. Surely to God he should have at least given me a Hail Mary or an Our Father to say fer penance."

She switched the subject abruptly. "But enough about that, girl. What are you doin' back this way?"

It was a question I had already asked myself several times, although I had only been back less than twenty-four hours. Nothing was as I had thought it would be. The cliffs weren't as bald, and the waves that lashed them smooth weren't as fierce as my memory had led me to believe. A gasoline service station stood in the spot that once had been the Protestant graveyard, which made me wonder what had happened to the two bodies that had been buried there.

Even the gravel roads had disappeared. They had splattered them with a mixture of oil and asphalt to keep the clouds of dust under control. That had disappointed me. I had wanted to smell the powder-fine dust that used to rise up with every gust of wind. I had wanted to taste the grit that would always coat my teeth in the aftermath of an eddy of sand and clay and dried grass and fallen twigs. And I had wanted my sandalled feet to feel the sharp rocks that used to always work their way to the surface and smash up hard and painful against an unprotected heel.

"I came back to look after my parents' graves," I said, nodding towards the cemetery in the distance. It was located on a high cliff overlooking the community. I suddenly remembered the terror I had felt on each occasion when I had followed a casket up the steep gravel road, afraid the vehicle carrying the body would sidle over the cliff. And I remembered stories from my childhood when horses had carried the caskets up that cliff and how on occasion they had baulked midway, refusing to go forward and how the pallbearers had to snake the rest of the way up the side of the cliff, lugging the casket on their shoulders.

Millie's dour-sounding voice broke me out of my reverie.

"Now, me darlin', there's heartbreak in store for you when ye goes up there." She gestured with a nod of her head toward the cemetery. "I can tell ye that much. They don't bury on the hill anymore, as you probably know. Got a new place. On the outskirts somewhere. On level ground. I went up on the Hill to tend to me husband's grave last week. Don't go often because I can't make that steep grade. All the graves along the side of the road – poor Wilf's and yer mudder's and fadder's and dozens of others – have all been taken over by alders. Such a tangled mess, my dear. Even the headstones have fallen over from the pressure of those bloody alder bushes."

When I met Mildred, I had been heading into the church. I had wanted to see if I could recapture the sense of serenity and peace that its interior had always been able to invoke in me. But now after hearing about the statues, the marble altar, the stained-glass windows, and the strange priest, that hope was dashed. Still, I took my leave of her and went in anyway.

I pushed open the heavy oak door that led into the cavernous vestibule of the church. I then went into the church proper and knelt down in a pew and looked around at the newly austere interior. I remembered how I used to visit the church, not just on Sundays, but on weekdays as well, especially on sunny days. I would kneel in a back pew and watch the shafts of sunlight stream in through the stained-glass windows. Like Christopher Robin saying his prayers, I would cover my eyes with my hands and peek out through my fingers. In the drab world in which I then lived – black uniforms, brown coats, grey mitts, palings and barns and dories licked bare by the beastly March winds – the bright reds, blues, yellows, greens, purples in the stained glass were breathtaking. I would become transported into another realm, one that was far beyond my fog-shrouded community.

Mesmerized by the dazzling colours I could easily believe in heaven. It was a place that was fog free. The houses would be freshly painted and no clapboards would be laid bare by the salty whitecaps that blew in over a narrow, leaky beach. The dwellers would be dressed in gauzy colourful clothing. There wouldn't be a grey mitt or black sock in sight. And no one would be trying to grow potatoes and turnips in soil so thin it was almost impossible to find enough to cover the seed. And of course there would be flower gardens galore, and with varieties of flowers that I had only seen in seed catalogues. Delicate flowers.

Not merely hardy ones like lilacs and wild roses.

After my visit to the church, I had intended to go see the house in which I had been born and raised. In actuality, I was going to see the piece of ground on which the house I had been born and raised in had once stood; the house itself had burned to the ground one winter's night when the chimney had caught fire. From photographs, I knew that only a lilac tree, long gone wild, and a concrete slab that my father had placed at the bottom steps of our front entrance remained to testify that a house, a home, a family had once occupied this space.

When I came out of the church, I began walking towards the cemetery. Words that Millie had said circled in my brain like seagulls circling the landwash after spying a dead fish.

"Everyt'ing changes, girl. Sometimes for the best. Sometimes not. 'Tis the way it 'tis." As I trudged up the steep, potholed road to the cemetery, I constructed a new cautionary tale: "You can go home again. But perhaps you shouldn't."

# The Conversion

Mother's conversion to Confederation with Canada was immediate and instantaneous and could be likened to Paul's conversion on the road to Damascus. In one blinding, falling moment, she eschewed the exhortations of the Roman Catholic bishops of Newfoundland, the gossip of the people of the village of Caplin Scull who said she was a traitor to her country, and the derision of her neighbours who said she had become an Antichrist, just like Joey Smallwood himself.

Up until 1948, Mother's knowledge of Newfoundland politics was not only limited; it was jaundiced as well. There were two forms of governing power for the island, and both forms were made up of robbers. There was Responsible Government, which consisted of politicians who were homegrown robbers – the St. John's merchant barons. There was Commission Government, which consisted of politicians from

England who had been sent to Newfoundland to gov-
ern its tiny colony in the Atlantic Ocean. These she
referred to as foreign robbers. Adding to this cynical
view was her fervent belief that Newfoundland was
beyond the help of politicians, no matter what the
stripe. Having been born upon the godforsaken rock
meant you were fated to live hard and die hard and
with the great possibility of going to hell afterward.

When the issue of Newfoundland becoming the
tenth province of Canada rose, Mother found herself in a political dilemma. Although she surmised
that Confederation with Canada would offer a better future for the Newfoundlander, there was a hitch:
Canada was an unknown entity and as such teaming
up with this country ran counter to her oft-stated
maxim "The divil you know is better than the divil
you don't know."

Adding to her dilemma was her awareness that a
vote for Confederation meant opposing the command
of the bishop of her dioceses. It meant opposing almost all of the bishops in all of the dioceses in Newfoundland. The bishops not only counselled from the
pulpit, but disseminated encyclicals throughout the
dioceses as well, advising their flock to vehemently
oppose Confederation with Canada.

The encyclicals sent out by the diocese proclaimed that Canada was a heathen country and predicted that if Confederation with Canada became an
actuality, the presently operated parochial schools
in Newfoundland – in particular Roman Catholic –
would become a thing of the past. A further exten-
sion of this firmly held belief stated that even schools
owned and operated by the various other religions

in the province would be quickly replaced by secular-run ones as well. Because a Christian parochial school of any faith trumped a secular, ungodly Canadian government-run school, it was stated that a vote for Confederation was not only a vote against Catholicism; it was a vote against Christianity itself.

A letter from her son who was working in Gander – a small, newly constructed town in Central Newfoundland – set aside all of her misgivings. Alan, her first-born and, not to be denied, a very intelligent young man, extolled the rewards that would come to Newfoundland if it became part of Canada. Included in the letter was a snapshot of himself and Joey Smallwood. In the picture the two of them sported bow ties and dress suits, the bow ties appearing to be too big for their equally small frames. Both Joey and Alan were holding up handmade signs that read: All out for Confederation! This clinched it for Mother.

The instant she looked at that picture, she became a Confederate. "Joey" – she already had begun to refer to him by his first name, and reverentially – had an honest face and with that pronouncement she accepted the mantle of "Confederate" with all of the zeal of a born-again Christian. Everyone in our village soon became acquainted with her political bent of mind and none more so than Aloysious, her next-door neighbour, who was a zealot for Responsible Government.

In the course of tending to his farm animals, Aloysious had to pass by our house several times a day – to water his cattle, to milk his cows, to draw drinking water from our common well. It was a rare day that he did not drop in for a cup of tea or to bring baked goods his wife had sent along to us children, or just to exchange the day's news of the village. The two of them had been friends and neighbours all of their married lives.

After Mother's conversion the nature of these drop-ins changed radically. While previously the conversation had always revolved around village chitchat, who got drunk, who got laid off, what the priest said in his sermon on Sunday, whether the constant rain was going to make the potatoes rot in the ground, or whether Jack's Jim's sheep were going to freeze to death because he sheared them too early, it now centred on hurling insults at one another, sometimes camouflaged, sometimes not so much, regarding their unwise political affiliations. Not a visit went by without some scornful denunciation of Confederation with Canada or a caustic remark by Mother about the corruption of the St. John's merchants who were gouging the poor fishermen out of every penny they earned.

"Heard Antichrist on the radio last night. Talking tripe as usual," Aloysious would say, getting the conversation underway. He would be referring to Joey Smallwood and his radio program, *The Barrel Man*.

To this Mother would respond, "And he sure gave it to that divil, Cashin. He made no bones about saying how he had robbed the poor fishermen and is now setting himself up to rob the whole Island. And he predicted if we vote Responsible Government, we'll all end up back on the dole like in the Dirty Thirties."

"At least I won't end up in hell like you for selling our country to the heathens," Aloysious would respond.

On one particular Tuesday, the day of the weekly mail delivery, everyone in the village received a large, approximately twenty-four-inch-square, glossy photograph of Smallwood. It was so large it completely covered one of the two panes of glass in our parlour window, which is where Mother chose to display it. She knew Aloysious was bound to see it when he passed by our house as he came and went to do his farm chores.

As soon as the picture was in place, Mother went out to view it to see how eye-catching it would be for Aloysious. But as she went down the porch steps she stumbled and had to right herself by grabbing the wooden railing. It was then that she saw what had caused her to stumble. It was the glossy picture of Joey Smallwood that Aloysious had placed there. Only he had done more than just place it there. He had stapled his picture of Smallwood to a stiff piece of cardboard. He then lopped off Joey's head and with the help of rabbit wire, substituted the head of a recently caught herring. He had made certain, however, that the bow tie was visible.

Most people would have considered it to be ridiculously funny. Not Mother. It was sacrilegious. The insult was so severe that she spent the rest of the morning trying to forge a plan that would trump Aloysious' dastardly deed. Finally, she came up with one.

In every home in Caplin Scull – Roman Catholics all – it was the practice to hang a crucifix on the door that immediately came into view whenever anyone entered the home. In our house this door was the one leading from our kitchen into our parlour.

Our crucifix was large. It was made of wood, painted black, and it had a silver Christ suspended upon it, complete with bloodied feet, hands, and side. It also had a large metal clasp on the back of the crossbar. This clasp was slipped over a nail that had been driven in the centre of the parlour door. Whenever our back door was yanked open or banged shut – the need for and force of both the yanking and the banging depended upon the force of the unceasing wind – the crucifix would swing back and forth on its clasp. Sometimes it swung gently. Most times it swung furiously.

Mother had decided that the perfect insult to Aloysious would be to remove this crucifix and hang Joey's picture in its place. Because it was Saturday and both my younger brother and I were present, she felt the need to account for the blasphemous act she was about to commit.

"Sure, 'tis jest a bit of fun," she said in her thick Newfoundland Irish brogue. "Jest to torment him. He's crucifying Joey and I can't let him get off with that."

With the picture in place, she immediately started preparing the noon-hour meal. All the while she was working, she kept taking quick glances out through the kitchen window, impatiently waiting for Aloysious to come up the porch steps.

Now as it so happened, this was the time of year for the priest to visit each family in the village to collect his tithe. The ritual – in place for many years – was that on a Monday he would visit the families who lived up the road. On a Tuesday he would visit the families who lived up the pond and on a

Wednesday he would visit the families who lived over the road.

Because it was Saturday and because we lived over the road, Mother knew she had plenty of time to prepare for the priestly visit. She would have to dust the parlour, pry open the front door because it always stuck on account of the dampness, and make certain there would be no unsavoury cooking odours in the house.

With the salt beef already boiling in a pot on the stove, the potatoes ready to be added, she started preparing the cabbage. Just as she was crossing the floor to place the cabbage in the pot, she heard footsteps. Certain it was Aloysious, she cautioned us not to look at the door where the crucifix had once hung. She wanted him to find it for himself. She glanced out the window. It was not Aloysious who was coming up the steps! It was the new priest who had recently come to the parish to relieve our older priest. Apparently he had not been drilled on the proper format for visiting the homes for tithing.

In a total fluster, Mother started for the porch, cabbage in hand. She dropped the cabbage on the table. Then she realized her apron had gotten dirty when she had wiped her hands on it after she had peeled the potatoes. She pulled it off and stuffed it under a cushion. At a glance she saw the cluttered kitchen. The table still had dishes from breakfast. And there was the smell of salt beef cooking.

"Sweet Jesus, Mary, and Joseph," she said as she hurried to open the kitchen door and then the porch door. "Me house is a mess!"

At the last instant she remembered that Smallwood's picture was hanging in the space reserved for the crucifix.

"Get the crucifix back! Get the crucifix back!" she hissed at my brother as she hurried to answer the priest's knock.

My brother, who was only seven at the time, scrambled for the crucifix to rehang it. This he did. What he did not do, however, was remove Smallwood's picture before he re-hung it and he simply hung the crucifix over Joey's smiling face. Mother left the door between the kitchen and porch open behind her.

As was usual, there was a gale-force wind outside. Pulling the back door open and then having to slam it shut after the priest had entered caused the crucifix to swing madly back and forth across Smallwood's face. With each swing one of Smallwood's eyes was covered and the other one exposed. It looked like he was winking. A demonic wink! Each swing also exposed one corner of Smallwood's lips, while the other corner was covered with the crossbar of the crucifix. You could tell from a glimpse of his upturned partially exposed mouth that Joey was smiling. A lopsided, demonic smile!

We all stared as if transfixed at the winking and smiling, winking and smiling Joey. Mother found her voice.

"Sit here, Fadder," she said, pulling out a chair from beside the table. The priest made no attempt to sit down. He kept staring at the swinging crucifix as if mesmerized. Finally, he burst out laughing, permitting my brother and me to laugh as well. But Mother did not laugh.

"I'll explain, Fadder," she said nervously. She went on to tell him about her friendly feud with Aloysious over Confederation, about him replacing Joey's head with the head of a herring, about her need to get back at him. And then almost in the same breath, afraid that she would be considered disloyal to the Church, she hotly defended Confederation for an altruistic reason, saying it would be good for the children's future.

"I don't care what ye thinks of me, Fadder. I'm a Confederate through and through."

The more she explained, the more the priest laughed. When he sobered up, he said, "I can't wait to tell my mother about this. She'll get a kick out of it. She's a Confederate, too. But on the sly!"

## The Magic Box

I struggled to keep pace with my brother, Alan. My short, eight-year-old legs cut narrow, wavering furrows in the deep, freshly fallen snow. The wind whipped at my cheeks and the drifting snow spilled chillingly over the tops of my boots. But I was far too excited to feel any discomfort.

It was Saturday. The day the mail came. It was also the day that Alan was going to be getting the magic box. Or so we hoped. It was being sent to him by the Gold Medal Seed Company in thanks for him having sold Gold Medal Seeds.

It had to come today! The mail only came to Caplin Scull once a week and I could not wait seven more days. Alan had ordered his gift February 7, 1942. I knew the precise date of the order because I had leaned over his shoulder while he had written the letter and my eyes had followed every stroke of his pen.

The magic box had been pictured on the back page of the Gold Medal Seed Catalogue. The lid gaped open. I could see every thing that was tantalizingly spilling over its edge, exposing items so numerous and so marvellous that they fairly took my breath.

In my imagination the box was the size of the steamer trunk that was upstairs in the hall where my mother kept her woolen blankets. Alan had tried to bring down my expectations by saying it would prob-ably be the size of a shoebox. I hotly disagreed. There was no way a shoebox could hold all of the stuff mentioned, no matter how tightly it was packed.

There were pens that wrote with invisible ink, paper that glowed in the dark, packs of playing cards, dice with red dots, dice with black dots, and a book that promised to teach the lucky owner over one hun-dred magic tricks. There was even a magician's hat. It was turned upside down and filled with silk scarves of every colour in the rainbow. Below all of these wonders there was a message written in large black letters: FREE FOR SELLING ONLY TWENTY DOLLARS WORTH OF GOLD MEDAL SEEDS.

I had helped Alan sell the seeds, trudging from door to door, cajoling relatives and neighbours into buying packets of nasturtiums and marigolds and pansies and sweet peas even though those people had little time or money to put into such frivolity as growing delicate flowers that required constant at-tention. Besides, every inch of rocky land was needed to grow potatoes and cabbage and turnips, the staple diet of the villagers.

In return for helping him sell the seeds, Alan had promised to teach me how to do magic tricks.

The prospect of him imparting this knowledge to me filled me with such excitement that I had begun to ask him when the box would come even before he had sent his qualifying seed orders with the money order in the mail.

"I don't know any more than you do," he would say crossly, irked by my constant asking. "It has to come from Canada."

One day he brought an atlas home from school so he could trace all the stops and transfers involved in getting the magic box from Canada to Caplin Scull. All I knew about Canada was that the Lunenburg schooners came from there every spring to fish for cod and herring. Whenever a storm came up these schooners would head for the harbour that was less than a quarter of a mile from our house. On those occasions I would always sit by the kitchen window to watch as they headed for safety, their big white sails flapping in the wind.

Each time we went to collect the mail I would cry when the package hadn't arrived. Each time Alan would scold me.

"Stop that stupid crying," he would say. "You've got to pretend you don't care. That's what I do."

"But it hurts," I would wail. "I can't pretend it don't."

Finally, another mail day came around. I was up and ready to go long before the mail was due to be brought to the post office. But Alan was still in bed. He had been sick all week.

I started to go to his bedroom to wake him, but Mother waylaid me.

"Alan's too sick to get out of bed today. Last

night he took a turn for the worst and we have to get the doctor to him. You'll have to go to the post office by yourself."

Severely disappointed, I began to argue that it couldn't hurt him just to go to the post office, but Mother shushed me down the stairs. Sulkily, I got dressed and headed out. The sun danced on the snow as I rushed over the road. It made my shadow tease me into having a race with myself. I took heart in knowing that if the magic box came, it would make Alan feel better and he could begin teaching me the magic tricks before the day was out.

"There's a package here for Alan," Mrs. Margaret, the postmistress, said, her head poking out from an open shutter which she called a wicket. "I'm surprised he's not with you."

"He's sick," I said. "A cold settled in his lungs." I grabbed the package and rushed out the door. Like I had imagined all along, objects rattled and rolled around inside. I tore off for home.

I ran into the house and was about to go upstairs when my father stopped me.

"Can't go up there right now. The doctor just came."

"But I got the magic box," I said, as if that would have the power to cure Alan and the doctor would no longer be needed.

"Not now!" Father said sternly. "Not now! Put his package away for later."

"But ..."

"No buts. Put the box away for now!"

I angrily tossed the box into a nearby cupboard. Things rattled around when it landed on the shelf, but I paid no heed. It was only a box of useless junk. Like Mother had said, it would have been far better if Alan had ordered something sensible, like pencils and scribblers.

I went outdoors, slamming the door behind me, and I began to make snowballs with the sun-warmed snow. I shouted at the top of my voice, "I don't care! I don't care! I don't care! It's only a box of useless junk!" With the back of my mitten, I hastily brushed away rivulets of tears that were streaming down my cold cheeks.

## *The Lost Dory*

It was late fall, 1935. Ben, aged fourteen, together with his friend, Paul, had decided to take Ben's father's dory out on the Atlantic Ocean one last time before the sea got really rough, as it always did at that time of year. They had taken the dory out many times over the course of the summer – always on the sly because both boys feared the old man's wrath should he catch them moving the dory from its secure berth, high on the beach. *Never touch the dory without me being on hand!* That was one commandment that had been hammered home to both of them.

But they desperately needed tobacco and the only way to get money to buy a can of Prince Albert was to catch a codfish or two to sell in the village. And the only way to get a codfish was to take out the dory and hope to jig a couple of cod. They had tried it the day before, after Ben's father returned from fishing himself. By then the waves were high and treacherous and there was little time so they caught nothing. They had high hopes for today because they had stayed out long enough on other occasions to jig a codfish large enough to sell and get enough money to cover the cost of a can of Prince Albert and with enough left over to buy a box of Sea Dog matches.

Ben's father, always a cantankerous man, had become even more cantankerous since he had lost his berth on a whaling vessel that had plowed the Bermuda waters. Losing his berth meant he was now forced to do inshore fishing in his dory – an unmanly and shameful occupation which he considered just slightly above being a hangashore, someone too cowardly or too lazy to even put out to sea in a dory, or work on a whaling ship for that matter. But he consoled himself by saying that at least the dory allowed him to earn a modest living.

In their anxiousness to get a smoke, Paul and Ben practically ran all the way over the roughly gravelled road to the beach. When they reached the crest, they quickly scanned the area for the bright green dory that always stood apart from the others – the dory they had pulled so high upon the beach yesterday that it was well out of reach of the high tide which could pull it out to sea. They saw black dories. They saw yellow dories. They saw red dories. But they did not see a green dory. They looked out to the ocean. Had it been out there bobbing around in the waves, they would have taken another dory to rescue it. But the great expanse of ocean was empty. They scanned the beach again. There was no green dory to be seen.

They began to second-guess themselves. Had they pulled it up far enough so that it was secure from the high tide that always occurred about three or four o'clock in the morning? In their anxiousness to get a fish so they could buy their tobacco, had they taken the time to make certain the dory had been pulled high enough to be completely out of danger? Obviously not! They scanned the ocean once again, hoping to see a green dory bobbing about in the waves. But there was none to be seen. Reluctantly, they admitted to each other they had lost the dory.

"What in the name of Christ are we going to tell yer father?" Paul asked worriedly, knowing there was nothing that could be said or done other than confessing to their wrongdoing. "He'll strangle us fer sure."

Ben answered lightly. "Not to worry, b'y. I'll say, 'Fadder, I lost yer dory' and he's so goddamn contrary he'll argue me I didn't. And I'll let it go at that. Or I might even say, 'Yer right, Fadder.' Ye knows how he loves being right."

Paul shook his head, not convinced. "Let's hope he's as contrary as you make him out to be," he said, "because as sure as hell that dory is now halfway to England."

# Little Boy Pink

Four-year-old Loretta waited impatiently for her seven-year-old brother Francis to come and escort her back to her own house. She had just seen him come out their back door to take the shortcut through the meadow. She was excited to be going home, even though she still could not understand why she had been sent to spend the night at her grandfather's house when her grandmother was spending the night at her house. While she waited, she scuffed her leaky boots in the wet, early spring grass. She could feel the cold water squish up between her toes.

Another thing Loretta could not understand was why her mother, or for that matter her grandmother, never gave her a straightforward answer when she would ask them a question, like when was she going to get new boots – ones that did not leak. At such times, her mother would stare across the room at the faded wallpaper or out through the window by the kitchen table and say in a far-away voice, "All in God's good time, my darling. All in God's good time."

Her grandmother had the same habit of answering. "When are you going to get a new Sunday dress, Grandma? This one has rips."

"All in God's good time, child. All in God's good time."

When Francis got within earshot of where Loretta was waiting, he shouted to her, "We have a new Momma doll. Same size as Loretta Anastasia."

Loretta squealed her delight. "I have two Loretta Anastasia's!"

He hedged. "Well, sort of. It's a baby and he's sick."

The gender of the newcomer did not matter to Loretta, but having two dolls at home did matter because now she could have her Loretta Anastasia all to herself. The new one could sit on the shelf in the parlour.

Last summer a relative from Boston had visited and she had brought a large doll for Loretta, a doll in a pink silk dress – but not just ordinary pink. Pink with a touch of lilac. Heliotrope, her mother said. She also had a silk coat to match. And a bonnet, too. With lace trim. Delicate, spidery lace that left a fine shadow on the doll's face.

When Loretta was asked to give the doll a name, she did not hesitate. "Her name is Loretta Anastasia. Same as my name."

Francis had protested, saying the doll should have a name of her own, but Loretta firmly repeated, "Her name is Loretta Anastasia!"

To her dismay, she was not allowed to carry the doll in her arms all day long. Her mother said she was too beautiful to be dragged about and the proper place for her was on the parlour shelf. She then removed a vase of faded paper flowers from the shelf and placed the doll there instead.

However, each night, just before bedtime, Loretta was allowed to hold the doll for a few minutes. These were exotic moments for a person who had experienced precious few of them, living as she did in a poverty-stricken village, in the Depression-burdened colony of Newfoundland in the mid 1930s.

\* \* \* \* \*

As soon as they got close to her house, Loretta rushed ahead of Francis and raced up the rickety porch steps and on into her kitchen. She was expecting everyone to be excited over the new doll or the new baby, whichever it was. Instead she felt only a heavy sadness. Mrs. Matilda, a neighbour, was visiting and she was cutting up a white pillowcase that she must have brought from her home because it had embroidery on it. In Loretta's household the pillowcases were not so fancy.

Her grandmother was covering an empty biscuit crate with the pieces of pillowcase that Mrs. Matilda handed to her. She carried on with a conversation that had begun earlier.

"'Cash,' he said. 'Only cash!' He had all the turnips he could use. He might have been able to save the child."

Without taking her eyes from the pillowcase, Mrs. Matilda answered, "Some doctor he is! May he rot in hell when his time comes."

Loretta started to go upstairs. Her grandmother called her back.

"Don't go up there, child. The priest just came."

"Where's the baby?"

"In heaven. He didn't make it!"

Mrs. Matilda quickly laid the scissors aside and took hold of Loretta's arm. "I bet you'd like some fresh cream and partridgeberry jam for breakfast." She winked at her grandmother. "Come with me, and after breakfast I'll show you our new baby calf."

Reluctantly, Loretta went with Mrs. Matilda.

An hour later when she returned home, there was no one in the kitchen so she headed upstairs. To do so she had to pass by the parlour. The door was open. She went in. The pillowcase-covered biscuit box was on a table in the centre of the room and a burning candle was on either side of it. She peeked into the box. She saw a baby, its hands folded across its breast. The baby was dressed in a pink outfit – pink with a touch of lilac in it. Heliotrope perhaps! It was similar to Loretta Anastasia's outfit. In fact, it was so similar that Loretta immediately looked towards the shelf in the corner to be reassured that Loretta Anastasia was still there. And she was there, but a brown paper bag had been pulled over her head and body.

Loretta understood instantly and totally. She began to scream loudly. Wildly.

She clawed at the dead baby. "Take the clothes off him. Right now! They're Loretta Anastasia's!"

Her father and grandmother rushed to pacify her, finally doing so by convincing her that they had only borrowed the clothes – just until the neighbours saw "poor little Joseph" being waked. They assured her that Loretta Anastasia would get the outfit back the next day – as soon as they took Joseph to be buried.

Only slightly appeased, she demanded, "Promise! Cross your heart and hope to die!"

"Promise," they said in unison. Each one made the sign of the cross over their heart with their right thumb. "Promise!"

Loretta needed further assurance. "Say what Francis always says. Say 'Bless me, Father. I'll not lie. The devil will have me if I die.'"

They repeated her words verbatim.

* * * * *

Mrs. Matilda stayed the night and shortly after daylight she came to Loretta's bedroom to tell her she was going to be having breakfast at her house once more. Again Loretta reluctantly went with her, being neither hungry for the scalded cream and partridge-berry jam nor interested in the baby calf. Within the hour she insisted on going back home and no amount of coaxing would persuade her to stay.

On the way home she caught sight of her father and Mrs. Matilda's husband walking down her lane. Her father had the biscuit box on his shoulder. She knew they were taking the baby to be buried and that meant Loretta Anastasia could get her clothes back.

She ran home so fast that the wet spring grass sent sprays of cold water up her legs.

* * * * *

She ran straight into the parlour, pulled a chair over to the shelf where Loretta Anastasia sat wrapped in the brown paper bag. She ripped off the bag and stared stupefied at Loretta's still naked body.

Frantically, she began to search for her clothes. Under cushions. Behind tables. She searched the kitchen. She ran upstairs to her mother's bedroom. Her grandmother was there, sitting on the bed crying. Her mother was crying, too. Loretta barely noticed.

She eyeballed her grandmother. "Where's her clothes? I can't find her clothes." But even as she screamed, she knew why she could not find Loretta Anastasia's clothes: they were still on baby Joseph, who was on his way to be buried on Dixon's Hill.

"You lied! You promised!"

Her grandmother tried to explain why they had not kept their promise.

"His little arms," she said, extending her own arm to demonstrate, "got so stiff in those few hours. I couldn't bear to break them to get the clothes off. I just couldn't."

Loretta rushed downstairs and over to the shelf in the parlour where Loretta Anastasia sat. She pulled her down and held her naked body close. Then, to make her more comfortable, she placed her in a sitting position. When she did so, Loretta Anastasia opened her eyes. There was a question in them that only Loretta could interpret: "When am I going to get my clothes back?"

Again she hugged the doll even tighter to her body and looked off across the parlour, across the shabby chairs and the faded couch and in a far-away voice answered, "All in God's good time, my darling! All in God's good time!"

# The Lenten Sacrifice

If you were to mention Bertie Foley's name in the village of Caplin Scull, someone would be sure to say that he was "some queer hand." In village parlance, this meant that Bertie said things and did things most people would consider to be inappropriate, irreverent, or even outrageous. However, everyone would agree on one point: he never meant to deliberately harm or hurt anyone. His words and actions were just part of his peculiar nature.

The villagers would pass off Bertie's odd ways of acting and talking as Bertie being Bertie. For example, in the 1930s in the midst of the Great Depression, he spit his chew of tobacco into the Sunday collection basket instead of a monetary offering. He later explained to the priest that Joe Rowe had spitefully held the basket in front of his face a second or two longer than necessary just to humiliate him. Joe, he said, knew full well he did not have as much as two black coppers to place over his eyes should he die during the night. He had added, holding his eyes open with his fingers, "As I told the priest, 'I'll have to keep staring at those damn cobwebs on the parlour ceiling for the full three days and nights of me wake.'"

By village standards, Bertie wasn't much of a fisherman. They called him a hangashore because he refused to put out on the open sea in a dory if there was the slightest sign of a breeze. He said, as if it explained his cowardice, that he didn't relish becoming a meal for an ugly lobster, and invariably added that the first man who attempted to eat a lobster must have been some goddamn hungry.

For that matter, Bertie wasn't much of a farmer either. Instead of doing the back-breaking work of first clearing his land of rocks and dead stumps, he had settled for skirting tree trunks and boulders in order to plant his potatoes and turnips and cabbage gardens. Still and all, he usually harvested a crop that was sufficient to carry his family through the winter. A large family at that – so large they said he had to turn them outdoors to count them.

And he also wasn't much of a believer in religion, particularly in regards to sacrificing for Lent. He said it was a way the church had of nickelling and diming the last penny out of your pocket. They would put on a bazaar as soon as Lent was over on the off chance you had saved a penny or two by abstaining from meat or other expensive food. Knowing his bent of mind, it surprised the whole family, nay the whole village, when he made it known that his family, including himself, was going to be making a Lenten sacrifice. They were going to give up slathering churned butter on their bread for the upcoming forty days of Lent.

As it turned out, and as the villagers had correctly surmised, Bertie's demand for him and his household to abstain from butter had nothing at all to do with cleansing the soul or scourging the body. Many prophesized it was a scheme that somehow or in some way could be put to Bertie's advantage. To this end they were quite right.

A neighbour, who had recently agreed to board two new teachers who were coming to Caplin Scull for the spring months, had asked him if she could buy a couple of molds of freshly churned butter from him each week. He, of course, had eagerly agreed. Every few dollars helped. There was just one problem: there was never any butter left to sell. The family ate up every morsel his wife churned each week.

He hit upon on a plan. He would use the children's embarrassment over his lack of conforming to Church rules to his own advantage. He knew that Mary Ellen especially, who was fifteen, was embarrassed that he did not go to church or follow any of the rules of the Church, such as abstaining from eating meat on Fridays. Or going to Confession at least once a year. What if he were to pretend that he had become a sudden convert – converted to such an extent that he, too, was going to abstain from eating butter during Lent? He then could sell the unused butter to his neighbour and be able to pocket seven or eight dollars each month.

When he told the children of his intentions, there were groans and moans all around. He hastily pointed out that it was certainly a sacrifice for everyone. Instead of butter on their toast, he said, they could use blackstrap molasses – a cheap and foulsmelling treacle-like mixture, the bottom of the puncheon of molasses, which they all despised.

To answer their moans and groans, he asked, "Isn't it true that Jesus went without a morsel of food for forty days and forty nights?"

They mumbled that yes, it was true.

Delighted with himself that he was reeling them in, he pushed on. "And did He grouch and grumble?"

"No," they replied in unison.

"Then ye fellows have to stop kicking up a bloody fuss because ye have to go without butter for a few weeks."

The days without butter on their toast were interminable. Each day they marked it off on the calendar. A milestone in their minds. Sundays were ordinarily not counted as a Lenten day, but Bertie said that he was including them because it would be too easy to backslide if after six days they returned to the butter.

What he did not tell them, and what they did not know until the forty days were up, was that he had no intention of providing freshly churned butter for them at the end of Lent. He was simply going to tell them, "If you can go without butter on your bread for forty days, there is no reason why you can't go without it for another forty – or fifty."

Or for as long as they were under his roof.

# Do Not Substitute

Hilda Pike O'Connor sits at the table in her dimly lit kitchen furiously berating herself for her stupid mistake – a mistake that was going to make her the laughingstock of Caplin Scull – a mistake that was going to bring disgrace on Princess Sheila – a mistake that would make her son, who was coming home from Toronto for the New Year, ashamed of her.

How could she have made such a foolish error? She was certain she had ordered a settee for her parlour, but all that had been sent to her was a covering for a settee. And it had come in the mail – not at the train station as she had expected. At first she thought it was the fault of Eaton's. She was certain she had clearly written DO NOT SUBSTITUTE on the order. However, now that the covering has arrived and she has had a chance to double-check the catalogue, she has to admit she has misunderstood the advertising. How could she have believed she could have gotten a settee, the like of which was pictured in the catalogue, for only $49.95?

It was the first time she had ever ordered from the catalogue. In fact, it was the first time she had ever seen an Eaton's catalogue. As soon as the papers were signed in Ottawa that Newfoundland was going to be part of Canada, the catalogues had begun appearing in Caplin Scull and not just from Eaton's, but from a company called Simpson's and several others as well. They were all mesmerizing and tantalizing and carried the same message on their front cover: *Now duty free to Newfoundland.* It was heady stuff indeed!

Selena, Hilda's mother, God rest her soul, had brought Hilda up with the awareness that she was a direct descendent of Princess Sheila, an Irish princess who had landed in Mosquito Cove (later called Bristol Hope) in 1602. Selena's maiden name was Pike and she hailed from Bristol Hope, which was enough to convince her that she and Princess Sheila were closely related. To this end, Selena had passed on whatever skills she had to her daughter in the hope that she would grow up to make Princess Sheila proud.

As the story went – and some would say it is just that, a story – Princess Sheila had been a passenger on a French ship going to her native homeland – Ireland – when it was commandeered by a pirate ship that had been heading for Newfoundland. The captain's right-hand man on that ship was Gilbert Pike. During the course of the journey, Gilbert fell madly in love with the princess and he persuaded the captain to marry them on board ship. Here again the story diverges. Some say the captain was forced to marry them in order to stave off bad luck and the marriage had nothing to do with love. A single woman on a ship did not bode well.

Princess Sheila was skilled. She knew how to help birth babies, find medicines amongst the weeds growing in the meadows in Mosquito Cove. She could shear sheep, card the wool, and spin this wool into yarn from which she would knit sweaters and socks for her family, and for other families as well. On top of these accomplishments, she could read and write better than anyone else in her village.

Knowing all of Princess Sheila's accomplishments only served to tell Hilda she would be the laughing-stock of Caplin Scull when the news got round that she had ordered a settee and got a settee cover instead. And get around the news would because she would have to confess her mistake to the gossiping postmistress when she sent the cover back. It was unthinkable that anyone who maintained she was a relative of Princess Sheila would make such a stupid mistake. She quickly came to the conclusion that she just could not own up to it.

But how could she pass off the fact that she had ordered a settee cover instead of a settee? She pondered on this for a day or so and then arrived at a conclusion. She asked herself what Princess Sheila would do if she had to deal with such a situation. So she told herself that if the mountain would not come to the princess, the princess would go to the mountain. So she, Hilda, a direct descendent of that proficient Irish royal, would do likewise. She would build a settee to accommodate the cover! She would tell anyone who asked that she had ordered the covering purposely with this in mind.

Her recently dead husband had been a dory builder and he had a shed filled with tools. She knew how to use them; she had helped him build dories on many occasions. There was also plenty of lumber scattered about his shed. As well, she had bags of wool left over from the sheep-shearing in the spring which she could use as padding. She told herself that if she were to begin the project right away, she could have it completed by Christmas or soon thereafter. In time for Tom's visit!

She worked day and night on building the settee, barely taking the time to eat or sleep. One evening, as she was stuffing wool into the cushion covers, she heard the bell chiming. Startled, she looked over at the clock and remembered it was Christmas Eve. She decided to stop work and go to church for midnight Mass. She quickly put away her tools, primped her hair, pulled on her coat and boots, and headed for the church.

The choir was singing as she slid into a pew, picked up a hymn book, and joined in the singing, intermittently interjecting her own thoughts. *Adeste fideles, laeti triumphantes* ... Nothing like a bit of Latin. *Venite adoremus, Dominum.* Some glad I got that settee nearly finished. It'll be ready days before Tom gets home. *Venite adoremus, Dominum.* Princess Sheila would be so proud of me!

## *Broken Vows*

We kept the midnight-to-daylight wake vigil, my twelve-year-old cousin Barney and I – he ten years my junior. We sat in the parlour that had been spruced up for the occasion – freshly starched curtains, newly waxed linoleum, and because it was June, a bottle of water held fresh cuttings of purple lilacs. These had been placed on a small table at the head of the casket, squeezed in between a silver Christ on a black wooden cross and a lighted candle that had been blessed by the church on Candlemas Day.

Suddenly and apropos nothing in our conversation, Barney announced, "When I grow up there are four things I am never going to do. I am never going to drink. I am never going to get married. I am never going to leave Newfoundland. And I am never going to swear."

As he spoke, he held his hands in front of him, palms up as if anointing his words, and then he looked across the room at my father's casket resting on a makeshift bier of straight-backed, newly painted kitchen chairs. Perhaps he was thinking of the many times this gentle, soft-spoken man had reached out to him with love and kindness.

Barney died alone, in some small town in Alberta, his body having been ravished by long-term abuse of alcohol. In central Newfoundland, a wife and three children mourned his passing.

I have often wondered whether he ever learned to swear.

# *Acknowledgements*

I wish to offer my appreciation to my Tuesday night writing group for listening and suggesting and then listening some more. I want to thank Nancy Bauer, the leader of this group, who turned my stories inside out and upside down until they were ground down to their very essence. I especially wish to thank Fredericton writer Ana Watts, who took over the responsibilities of getting the stories "press ready" after I was hospitalized.

I also wish to thank The Canada Council and the Arts Board of New Brunswick for their monetary help with this undertaking.

"The Summer of Lannie Ramunski" and "Viewing Not Advised" were previously published in *A Charm Against the Pain: An Anthology of All New Writing From Newfoundland*. St. John's, NL: Flanker Press, 2006.

"The Farewell" was first published in *Newfoundland Quarterly* Spring 1985 Volume LXXX, Number 4.

"Do Not Substitute" appeared as "Mr. Eaton's – Only What I Ordered Please" in *Gifts to Last: Christmas Stories from the Maritimes and Newfoundland.* Selected by Walter Learning. Fredericton, NB: Goose Lane Editions, 1996.

"The Death Watch" is an excerpt (Chapter 1) from the novel *A Fit Month For Dying.* Fredericton, NB: Goose Lane Editions, 2000.

## *About the Author*

M. T. (Jean) Dohaney is the author of five novels, one memoir, and, most recently, this collection of short stories, *Caplin Scull: Chronicles from a New-foundland Outport on the Eve of Confederation*. She has all the necessary academic prerequisites to be a fine writer – BA (English Literature), BEd, MEd, and PhD (Education) – but her "unfailing ear for dialogue and use of dark humour to create characters almost too vibrant to be contained by the page" (*Quill and Quire*), are probably more useful. And although she didn't recognize it as an advantage as a child, she was born during the Depression into a family and culture of storytelling in the hardscrabble village of Point Verte, Newfoundland. When it was too stormy to go fishing, the men sat around the kitchen table and told tales. Her mother and grandmother, whom Jean claims "had more guts than a herring," told their share too.

She came to Fredericton as a bride when her

New Brunswick husband Walt enrolled in engineering at UNB. She and their two small children followed him through Canada, the United States, and England as he pursued his advanced degrees. In British Columbia she began to write as a respite from her domestic life. Back in Fredericton, her husband ensconced as UNB faculty, she set out on her own academic path toward teaching and writing.

Her first novel, *The Corrigan Women* (1988), met with great critical acclaim. But it is her poignant memoir, *When Things Get Back to Normal* (1989) – written following Walt's sudden death playing hockey – that is most popular and satisfying. It continues to prompt calls and letters from those helped through their own grief. Her many honours include the 1996 Thomas H. Raddall Atlantic Fiction Award for *A Marriage of Masks*, and the 2012 New Brunswick Lieutenant-Governor's Award for High Achievement in the Literary Arts.